THE BIG BOOK OF SEEK & FIND

Tony Tallarico

Kidsbooks®

www.kidsbookspublishing.com

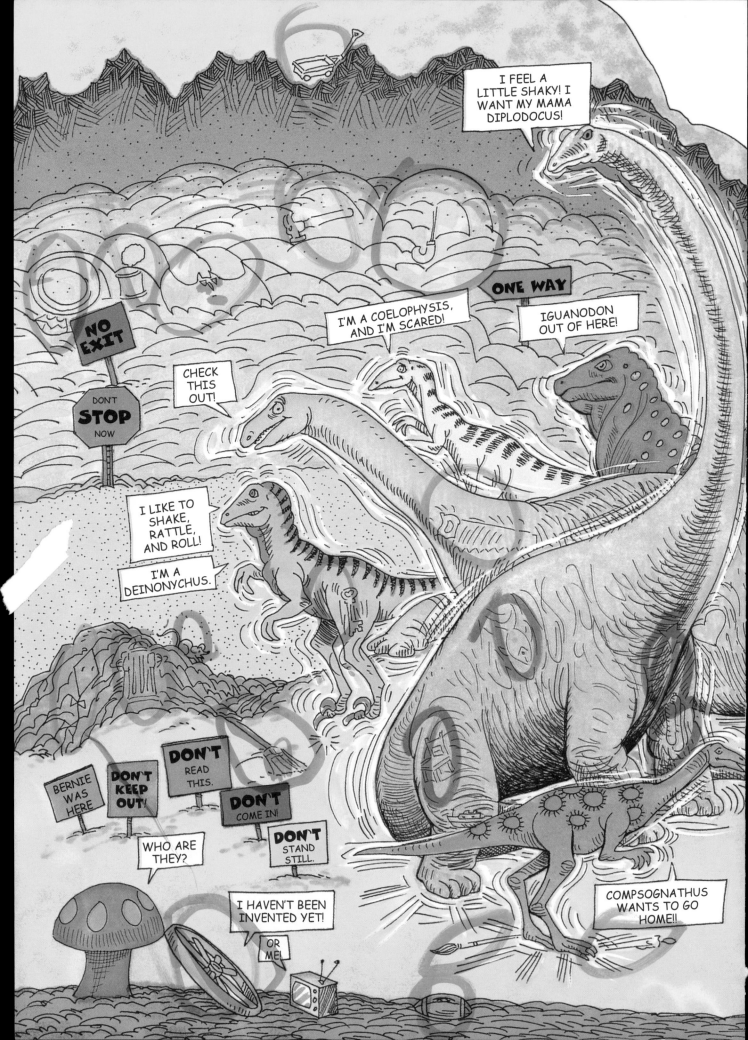

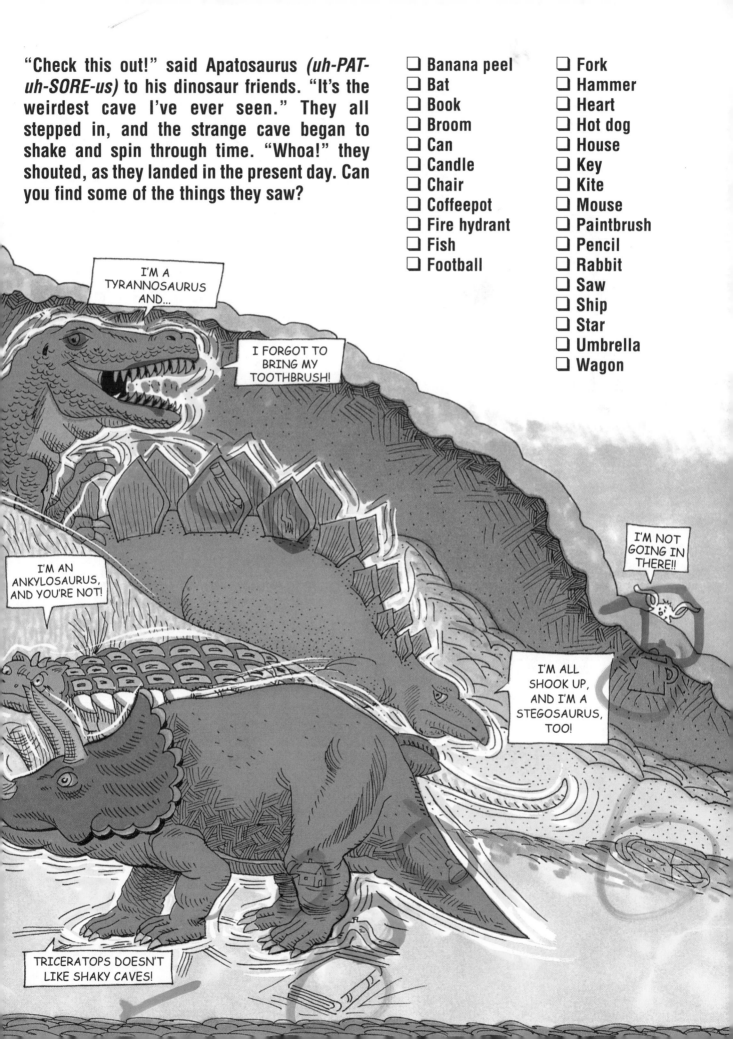

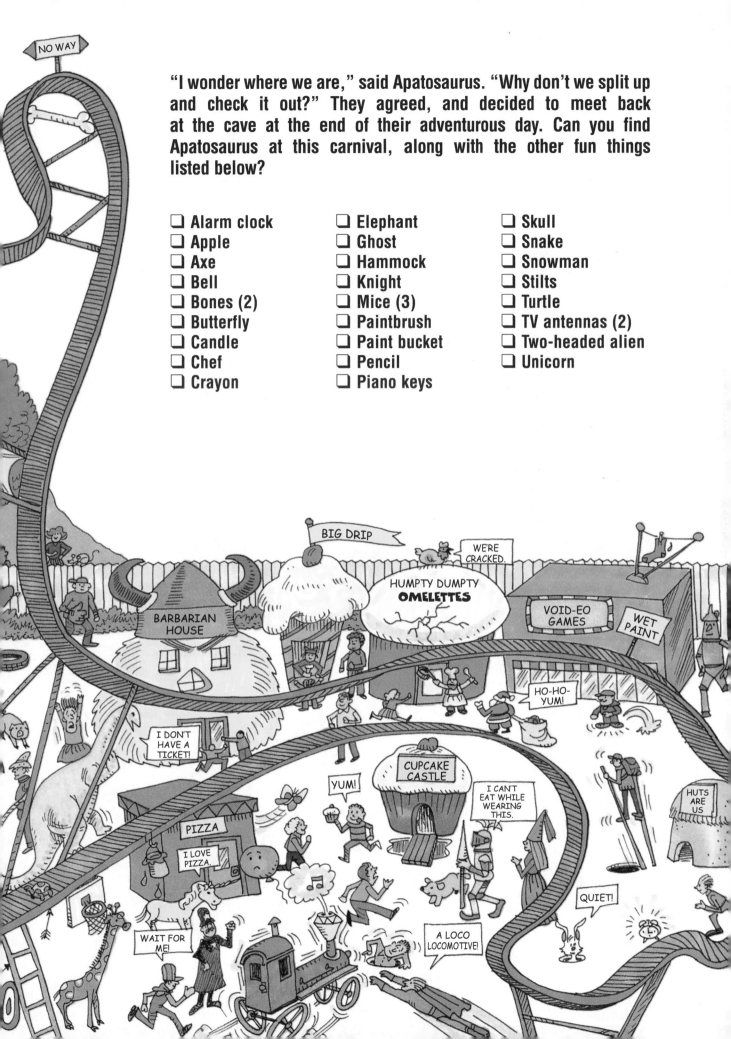

"I wonder where we are," said Apatosaurus. "Why don't we split up and check it out?" They agreed, and decided to meet back at the cave at the end of their adventurous day. Can you find Apatosaurus at this carnival, along with the other fun things listed below?

- ❑ Alarm clock
- ❑ Apple
- ❑ Axe
- ❑ Bell
- ❑ Bones (2)
- ❑ Butterfly
- ❑ Candle
- ❑ Chef
- ❑ Crayon
- ❑ Elephant
- ❑ Ghost
- ❑ Hammock
- ❑ Knight
- ❑ Mice (3)
- ❑ Paintbrush
- ❑ Paint bucket
- ❑ Pencil
- ❑ Piano keys
- ❑ Skull
- ❑ Snake
- ❑ Snowman
- ❑ Stilts
- ❑ Turtle
- ❑ TV antennas (2)
- ❑ Two-headed alien
- ❑ Unicorn

"This place sounds really crazy," said Compsognathus *(komp-sog-NAY-thus)*. "I wonder what's going on?" Can you find Apatosaurus and Compsognathus at this rock concert? Don't forget to look for the following fun things, too.

- ❑ Bell
- ❑ Birdcage
- ❑ Candle
- ❑ Chef's hat
- ❑ Chicken drumstick
- ❑ Crown
- ❑ Elephant
- ❑ Fish
- ❑ Hammer
- ❑ Heart
- ❑ Hot-air balloon
- ❑ Ice-cream cone
- ❑ Mermaid
- ❑ Mouse
- ❑ Octopus
- ❑ Owl
- ❑ Paper airplane
- ❑ Pencil
- ❑ Pie
- ❑ Rabbit
- ❑ Saw
- ❑ Skate
- ❑ Snail
- ❑ Sock
- ❑ Star
- ❑ Turtle
- ❑ Worm

"Oh, cool! But where am I?" said Triceratops *(try-SER-uh-tops)*. "Hey! I see some of my friends." Can you find Apatosaurus, Triceratops, and Compsognathus at this skating rink? Don't forget to look for the following fun things, too.

- ☐ Alligator
- ☐ Bone
- ☐ Bowling ball
- ☐ Broom
- ☐ Cactuses (2)
- ☐ Cameras (2)
- ☐ Crutch
- ☐ Elf
- ☐ Football player
- ☐ Humpty Dumpty
- ☐ Hungry monster
- ☐ Ice skateboard
- ☐ Igloo
- ☐ Kangaroo
- ☐ Lost mitten
- ☐ Mouse
- ☐ Necklace
- ☐ Panda
- ☐ Penguins (2)
- ☐ Pillow
- ☐ Roller skates
- ☐ Santa Claus
- ☐ Shark fin
- ☐ Skier
- ☐ Straw basket
- ☐ Telescope
- ☐ Television

"Yum! Something smells good," said Iguanodon *(ih-GWAHN-uh-don)*. "Maybe I'll give up eating plants." Can you find Apatosaurus, Triceratops, Compsognathus, and Iguanodon at this fast-food stand? Don't forget to look for the following fun things, too.

- Apple
- Astronaut
- Candy cane
- Chicken
- Clown
- Count Dracula
- Diver
- Doctor
- Dog
- Doughnut
- Duck
- Fish
- Monster
- Moose head
- Mouse
- Moustache
- Penguin
- Pinocchio
- Propeller
- Seal
- Star
- Straws (2)
- Surfer
- Torn bag
- Turtle
- Unicycle
- Viking

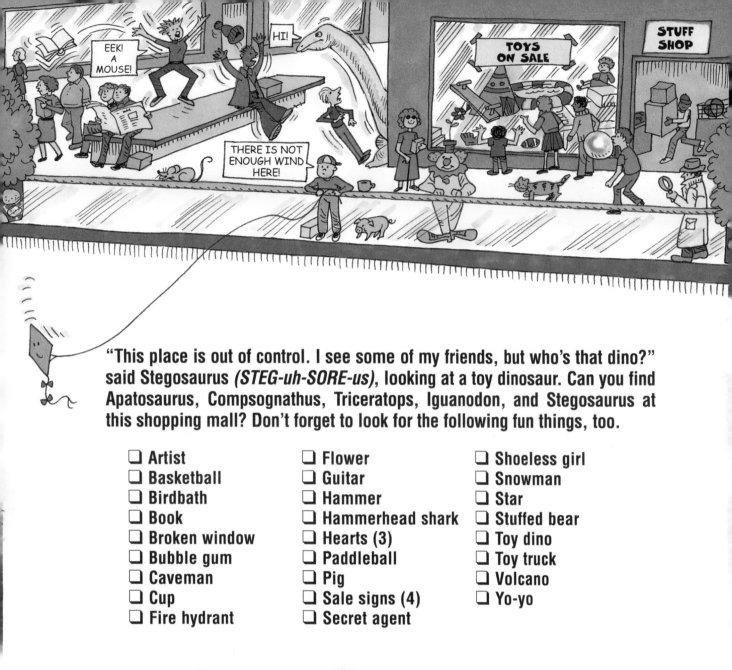

"This place is out of control. I see some of my friends, but who's that dino?" said Stegosaurus *(STEG-uh-SORE-us)*, looking at a toy dinosaur. Can you find Apatosaurus, Compsognathus, Triceratops, Iguanodon, and Stegosaurus at this shopping mall? Don't forget to look for the following fun things, too.

- ❏ Artist
- ❏ Basketball
- ❏ Birdbath
- ❏ Book
- ❏ Broken window
- ❏ Bubble gum
- ❏ Caveman
- ❏ Cup
- ❏ Fire hydrant
- ❏ Flower
- ❏ Guitar
- ❏ Hammer
- ❏ Hammerhead shark
- ❏ Hearts (3)
- ❏ Paddleball
- ❏ Pig
- ❏ Sale signs (4)
- ❏ Secret agent
- ❏ Shoeless girl
- ❏ Snowman
- ❏ Star
- ❏ Stuffed bear
- ❏ Toy dino
- ❏ Toy truck
- ❏ Volcano
- ❏ Yo-yo

"Look at all those little creatures! They seem to know where they're going," said Diplodocus *(dih-PLOH-duh-kus)*. "Maybe they can tell me where I am." Can you find Apatosaurus, Compsognathus, Triceratops, Iguanodon, Stegosaurus, and Diplodocus? Don't forget to look for the following fun things, too.

- ❏ Airplane
- ❏ Apple
- ❏ Arrow
- ❏ Balloons (3)
- ❏ Baseball
- ❏ Calendar
- ❏ Carrot
- ❏ Cat
- ❏ Coonskin cap

- ❏ Crown
- ❏ Elephant
- ❏ Football helmet
- ❏ Golf club
- ❏ Hockey stick
- ❏ Kites (2)
- ❏ Lunch box
- ❏ Oilcan
- ❏ Pyramid

- ❏ Rocket ship
- ❏ Roller skate
- ❏ Sailor hat
- ❏ Scissors
- ❏ Straw
- ❏ Unicorn
- ❏ Van
- ❏ Watering can

"Apatosaurus, Apatosaurus!" shouted Coelophysis *(SEEL-uh-FYE-sis)* to the statue. "Sorry, I thought you were my friend." Can you find Apatosaurus, Triceratops, Compsognathus, Iguanodon, Stegosaurus, Diplodocus, and Coelophysis at this amusing museum? Don't forget to look for the following fun things, too.

- ☐ Bird
- ☐ Boot
- ☐ Bowling ball
- ☐ Chef
- ☐ Fish
- ☐ Flying carpet
- ☐ Frog
- ☐ Hammer
- ☐ Headless body
- ☐ Ice-cream cone
- ☐ Jack-o'-lantern

- ☐ Lightbulb
- ☐ Mouse
- ☐ Mummy
- ☐ Pencil
- ☐ Periscope
- ☐ Piggy bank
- ☐ Pyramid
- ☐ Roller skates
- ☐ Rubber ducky
- ☐ Saw
- ☐ Screwdriver

- ☐ Soccer ball
- ☐ Swan
- ☐ Swords (2)
- ☐ Tic-tac-toe
- ☐ Tree stump
- ☐ Turtle
- ☐ TV antenna
- ☐ Upside-down picture

"I don't like this place at all," said Deinonychus *(dyne-ON-ik-us)*. "There are too many strange creatures. I'm getting out of here quick." Can you find Apatosaurus, Triceratops, Compsognathus, Iguanodon, Stegosaurus, Diplodocus, Coelophysis, and Deinonychus at this zoo? Don't forget to look for the following fun things, too.

- ❑ Aardvark
- ❑ Alien
- ❑ Anteater
- ❑ Arrow
- ❑ Baseball glove
- ❑ Bat
- ❑ Beaver
- ❑ Bighorn
- ❑ Bottle
- ❑ Butterfly
- ❑ Candle
- ❑ Clown
- ❑ Dog
- ❑ Duck
- ❑ Kangaroo
- ❑ Lost balloon
- ❑ Moose
- ❑ Net
- ❑ Owls (2)
- ❑ Panda
- ❑ Polar bear
- ❑ Raccoon
- ❑ Rhinoceros
- ❑ Sick animal
- ❑ Singing cactus
- ❑ Snakes (2)
- ❑ Toucan
- ❑ Umbrellas (3)
- ❑ Wolf
- ❑ Yak

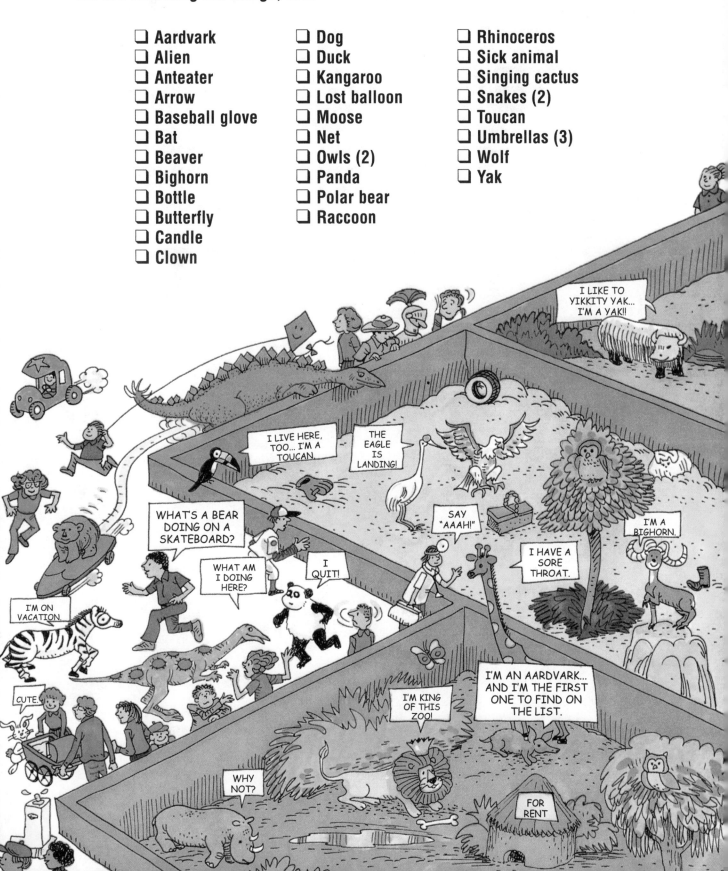

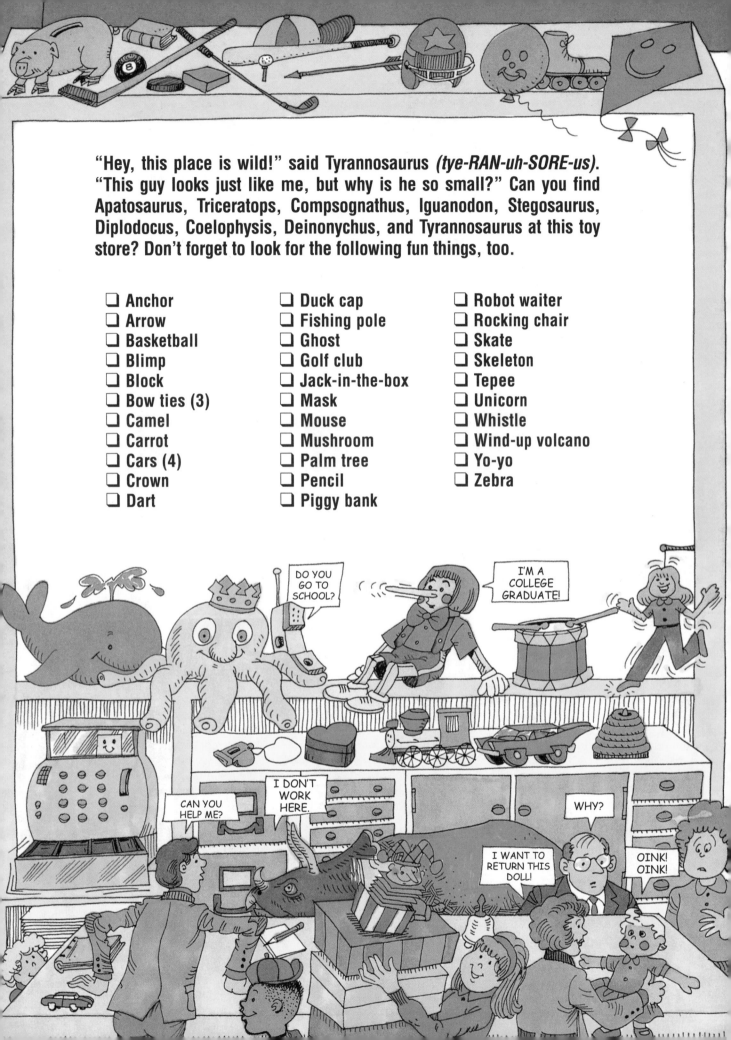

"Hey, this place is wild!" said Tyrannosaurus *(tye-RAN-uh-SORE-us)*. "This guy looks just like me, but why is he so small?" Can you find Apatosaurus, Triceratops, Compsognathus, Iguanodon, Stegosaurus, Diplodocus, Coelophysis, Deinonychus, and Tyrannosaurus at this toy store? Don't forget to look for the following fun things, too.

- Anchor
- Arrow
- Basketball
- Blimp
- Block
- Bow ties (3)
- Camel
- Carrot
- Cars (4)
- Crown
- Dart
- Duck cap
- Fishing pole
- Ghost
- Golf club
- Jack-in-the-box
- Mask
- Mouse
- Mushroom
- Palm tree
- Pencil
- Piggy bank
- Robot waiter
- Rocking chair
- Skate
- Skeleton
- Tepee
- Unicorn
- Whistle
- Wind-up volcano
- Yo-yo
- Zebra

"Oh, wow! What are those things flying in the air?" wondered Ankylosaurus *(an-KYE-low-SORE-us)*. Can you find Apatosaurus, Compsognathus, Triceratops, Iguanodon, Stegosaurus, Diplodocus, Coelophysis, Deinonychus, Tyrannosaurus, and Ankylosaurus at this big-balloon parade? Don't forget to look for the following fun things, too.

- ☐ Birds (2)
- ☐ Broom
- ☐ Candy cane
- ☐ Clown
- ☐ Coffeepot
- ☐ Cooking pot
- ☐ Cow
- ☐ Deflated balloon
- ☐ Fire hydrant
- ☐ Fish

- ☐ Giant
- ☐ Hammer
- ☐ Happy stars (5)
- ☐ Humpty Dumpty
- ☐ Ice skates (2 pairs)
- ☐ King Kong
- ☐ Kite
- ☐ Knight
- ☐ Lion
- ☐ Mouse
- ☐ Mummy
- ☐ Paintbrush

- ☐ Penguin
- ☐ Pirate
- ☐ Rabbits (2)
- ☐ Scarecrow
- ☐ Skier
- ☐ Sore feet
- ☐ Three Little Pigs
- ☐ Turtles (2)
- ☐ Unicyclist

Freddie and Lisa have discovered a house that is unlike any other—a haunted house!

FIND FREDDIE & LISA AT THE HAUNTED HOUSE, AND THESE FUN ITEMS:

- ☐ Apples (2)
- ☐ Baseball cap
- ☐ Bones (3)
- ☐ Box
- ☐ Burned-out candle
- ☐ Clothespin
- ☐ Coffeepot
- ☐ Crown
- ☐ Dog
- ☐ Duck
- ☐ Eyeglasses
- ☐ Faucet
- ☐ Fish tank
- ☐ Ghosts (3)
- ☐ Hammer
- ☐ Heart
- ☐ Kite
- ☐ Lips
- ☐ Mouse
- ☐ Owl
- ☐ Paint bucket
- ☐ Peanut
- ☐ Pencils (2)
- ☐ Piggy bank
- ☐ Saw
- ☐ Sock
- ☐ Submarine
- ☐ Truck
- ☐ Umbrella

Should they go in?
Should they stay in?
What do you think they
should do?

**FIND FREDDIE & LISA
BEFORE THEY DECIDE,
AND THESE FUN ITEMS:**

- ❏ Birds (2)
- ❏ Blimps (2)
- ❏ Bowling ball
- ❏ Broom
- ❏ Camel
- ❏ Candle
- ❏ Chef's hat
- ❏ Feather
- ❏ Flower
- ❏ Football
- ❏ Giraffe
- ❏ Jester
- ❏ King
- ❏ Laundry
- ❏ Lost boot
- ❏ Moustache
- ❏ Napoleon
- ❏ Painted egg
- ❏ Rabbit
- ❏ Red wagon
- ❏ Sailboat
- ❏ Short pants
- ❏ Skull
- ❏ Sled
- ❏ Slide
- ❏ Star
- ❏ Top hats (2)
- ❏ Trash can
- ❏ Umbrella

Ready, set, go! Everyone runs toward the door of the haunted house, but only two enter it!

FIND FREDDIE & LISA AS THEY MEET THE MONSTERS, AND THESE FUN ITEMS:

- ❏ Apple
- ❏ Arrow
- ❏ Bag
- ❏ Balloon
- ❏ Banana peel
- ❏ Baseball cap
- ❏ Bone
- ❏ Boot
- ❏ Broken heart
- ❏ Broom
- ❏ Cake
- ❏ Candles (5)
- ❏ Crystal ball
- ❏ Fish
- ❏ Genie
- ❏ Ghosts (2)
- ❏ Ice-cream cone
- ❏ Lightning
- ❏ Necktie
- ❏ Owl
- ❏ Piano
- ❏ Skulls (5)
- ❏ Snake
- ❏ Spoon
- ❏ Tombstone

Ms. Witch makes gross snacks. Her specialty is the "Everything Goes" sandwich!

FIND FREDDIE & LISA AT SNACK TIME, AND THESE FUN ITEMS:

- ☐ Accordion
- ☐ Apple
- ☐ Baseball
- ☐ Blackbird
- ☐ Bone
- ☐ Candle
- ☐ Checkerboard
- ☐ Drill
- ☐ Earring
- ☐ Fish (2)
- ☐ Flower
- ☐ Fork
- ☐ Frying pan
- ☐ Grapes
- ☐ Green cup
- ☐ Heart
- ☐ Helmet
- ☐ Ice-cream cone
- ☐ Ladle
- ☐ Neckties (2)
- ☐ Oilcan
- ☐ Orange
- ☐ Palm tree
- ☐ Pear
- ☐ Rolling pin
- ☐ Saw
- ☐ Sock
- ☐ Stool
- ☐ Toaster
- ☐ Wooden spoon

Freddie and Lisa begin to explore the haunted house. A wrong turn, and down they tumble!

FIND FREDDIE & LISA IN THE DUNGEON, AND THESE FUN ITEMS:

- ❏ Airplane
- ❏ Balloon
- ❏ Banana peel
- ❏ Bowling ball
- ❏ Broken egg
- ❏ Broom
- ❏ Candy cane
- ❏ Corn
- ❏ Cupcake
- ❏ Doctor
- ❏ Drum
- ❏ Fire hydrant
- ❏ Flowerpot
- ❏ Flying bat
- ❏ Football
- ❏ Hot dog
- ❏ Ice-cream cone
- ❏ Ice-cream pop
- ❏ Mummies (3)
- ❏ Piggy bank
- ❏ Rabbit
- ❏ Roller skates
- ❏ Scarecrow
- ❏ Shark
- ❏ Skateboard
- ❏ Skulls (2)
- ❏ Skunk
- ❏ Top hat
- ❏ Umbrellas (2)
- ❏ Wagon

Next to the dungeon are the wildest lanes in town. It's a great place to do anything—but bowl!

FIND FREDDIE & LISA AT THE GHOSTLY BOWLING ALLEY, AND THESE FUN ITEMS:

- ❏ Arrow
- ❏ Balloon
- ❏ Bird
- ❏ Bodiless head
- ❏ Broken ball
- ❏ Broom
- ❏ Cactus
- ❏ Candles (2)
- ❏ Carrot
- ❏ Dog
- ❏ Earphones
- ❏ Flower
- ❏ Hamburger
- ❏ Hot dog
- ❏ Mouse
- ❏ Mummy
- ❏ Mummy's ball
- ❏ Orange
- ❏ Pear
- ❏ Periscope
- ❏ Robot
- ❏ Sailboat
- ❏ Snowman
- ❏ Spring
- ❏ Sunglasses (2 pairs)
- ❏ Sword
- ❏ Tennis racket
- ❏ Tombstone
- ❏ Yo-yo

Dr. Frankenstein has lots of patients who need lots of patience.

FIND FREDDIE & LISA IN DR. FRANKENSTEIN'S LABORATORY, AND THESE FUN ITEMS:

- ❏ Black cat
- ❏ Book
- ❏ Bride
- ❏ Bunny fiend
- ❏ Candle
- ❏ Cheese
- ❏ Dog
- ❏ Dracula
- ❏ Duck
- ❏ Feather
- ❏ Greeting card
- ❏ Ice-cream pop
- ❏ Invisible person
- ❏ Paintbrush
- ❏ Paint bucket
- ❏ Pickax
- ❏ Roller skates
- ❏ Sailor fiend
- ❏ Saw
- ❏ Screwdriver
- ❏ Shovel
- ❏ Skull
- ❏ Suspenders
- ❏ Television
- ❏ Three-legged thing
- ❏ Toy block
- ❏ Tulip
- ❏ Two-headed thing
- ❏ Watch

After dinner, Freddie and Lisa explore a room upstairs. There they find someone who *really* knows how to save!

FIND FREDDIE & LISA IN DRACULA'S ATTIC, AND THESE FUN ITEMS:

- ❏ Boomerang
- ❏ Broom
- ❏ Candy cane
- ❏ Chef's hat
- ❏ Clocks (2)
- ❏ Cracked mirror
- ❏ Fire hydrant
- ❏ Garden hose
- ❏ Golf club
- ❏ Ice-cream cone
- ❏ Key
- ❏ Mouse
- ❏ Necklace
- ❏ Oar
- ❏ Paint bucket
- ❏ Paper airplane
- ❏ Pencil
- ❏ Pyramid
- ❏ Saw
- ❏ Skateboard
- ❏ Skulls (4)
- ❏ Slice of pizza
- ❏ Spray can
- ❏ Straw
- ❏ String of pearls
- ❏ Stuffed panda
- ❏ Telephone booth
- ❏ Viking helmet
- ❏ Yarn

The monsters walk very carefully when they visit *this* room!

FIND FREDDIE & LISA IN THE COBWEB ROOM, AND THESE FUN ITEMS:

- ❑ Baby carriage
- ❑ Binoculars
- ❑ Bow tie
- ❑ Boxing glove
- ❑ Broom
- ❑ Cup
- ❑ Dog
- ❑ Duck
- ❑ Earring
- ❑ Electric plug
- ❑ Fish
- ❑ Flower
- ❑ Football helmet
- ❑ Fork
- ❑ Ghosts (2)
- ❑ Hammer
- ❑ Heart
- ❑ Key
- ❑ Lock
- ❑ Mummy
- ❑ Old-fashioned radio
- ❑ Pencil
- ❑ Quarter moon
- ❑ Ring
- ❑ Robot
- ❑ Screwdriver
- ❑ Ship
- ❑ Skull
- ❑ Top hat
- ❑ Turtles (2)
- ❑ Wagon

Playtime for monsters!

FIND FREDDIE & LISA IN THE MONSTERS' PLAYROOM, AND THESE FUN ITEMS:

- ❏ Artist
- ❏ Balloon
- ❏ Banana peel
- ❏ Barbell
- ❏ Birds (2)
- ❏ Blackboard
- ❏ Crayons (5)
- ❏ Donkey
- ❏ Fish
- ❏ Football
- ❏ Haunted house
- ❏ Hole in the head
- ❏ Hood
- ❏ Ice skate
- ❏ Jack-o'-lanterns (4)
- ❏ Joke book
- ❏ Juggler
- ❏ Mask
- ❏ Monster puppet
- ❏ Mummy doll
- ❏ Musician
- ❏ Nail
- ❏ Pail
- ❏ Pogo stick
- ❏ Rubber ducky
- ❏ Sailboat
- ❏ Snake
- ❏ Telephone
- ❏ Tricycle
- ❏ Turtle
- ❏ Wind-up monster

It is time for Freddie and Lisa to go. The friendly monsters hope their new friends will return soon.

FIND FREDDIE & LISA LEAVING THE HAUNTED HOUSE, AND THESE FUN ITEMS:

- ❑ Apple
- ❑ Arrow
- ❑ Balloon
- ❑ Birds (2)
- ❑ Box
- ❑ Broken heart
- ❑ Brooms (2)
- ❑ Candles (2)
- ❑ Clock
- ❑ Crown
- ❑ Dog
- ❑ Duck
- ❑ Envelope
- ❑ Flower
- ❑ Ice skates
- ❑ Key
- ❑ Ladder
- ❑ Lamp
- ❑ Mouse
- ❑ Painted egg
- ❑ Periscope
- ❑ Quarter moon
- ❑ Rabbit
- ❑ Roller skates
- ❑ Shovel
- ❑ Skull
- ❑ TV camera
- ❑ Umbrella

In the old house was an old trunk, which the children opened with an old key. Out of the trunk came many strange things, including these hidden objects:

- ❏ Arrow
- ❏ Balloon
- ❏ Bearded man
- ❏ Carrot
- ❏ Chicken
- ❏ Fish
- ❏ Giraffe
- ❏ Horse
- ❏ Kite
- ❏ Mouse
- ❏ Quarter moon
- ❏ Snowman
- ❏ Tepee
- ❏ Tombstone
- ❏ Turtle
- ❏ Unicorn

Did you ever see such a sight in your life? It's not three blind mice—it's monsters! Monsters can be found everywhere, along with the following hidden pictures. Can you find them all?

- ❏ Arrow
- ❏ Automobile
- ❏ Candle
- ❏ Candy canes (2)
- ❏ Clothespin
- ❏ Comb
- ❏ Drum
- ❏ Evergreen tree
- ❏ Fish
- ❏ Flower
- ❏ Football
- ❏ Hairbrush
- ❏ Hot dog
- ❏ Kangaroo
- ❏ Key
- ❏ Locket
- ❏ Mouse
- ❏ Pen
- ❏ Pencil
- ❏ Skateboard
- ❏ Sock
- ❏ Tent
- ❏ Umbrella

In another room in the old house, the two kids found an ancient family album. Whose pictures do you think were inside? Before you can open it, you must find the following objects.

- ❏ Arrow
- ❏ Banana
- ❏ Bear
- ❏ Cactus
- ❏ Cane
- ❏ Cat
- ❏ Deer
- ❏ Fork
- ❏ Frog
- ❏ Giraffe
- ❏ Heart
- ❏ Ice-cream cone
- ❏ Monkey
- ❏ Mouse
- ❏ Owl
- ❏ Pencil
- ❏ Pig
- ❏ Rabbit
- ❏ Ring
- ❏ Rooster
- ❏ Saw
- ❏ Skull
- ❏ Snake
- ❏ Star

Wow! What a surprise! It is a photo album full of monsters! On the first page, there is a picture of young Frankenstein on his first date. Do you know which monster is on the next page? Before you look, find the following hidden objects:

- ❏ Airplane
- ❏ Automobile
- ❏ Butterfly
- ❏ Camera
- ❏ Candle
- ❏ Cup
- ❏ Drum
- ❏ Eyeglasses
- ❏ Fish
- ❏ Hearts (4)
- ❏ House
- ❏ Kite
- ❏ Lightbulb
- ❏ Owl
- ❏ Pencil
- ❏ Ring
- ❏ Rocket
- ❏ Sailboat
- ❏ Snake
- ❏ Surfboard
- ❏ Sword
- ❏ Tent
- ❏ Toothpaste
- ❏ Tree
- ❏ Turtle
- ❏ Umbrella
- ❏ Whistle

Wasn't Count Dracula a cuddly little critter? He loved to hide things. Can you find everything that he has hidden?

- ❏ Carrot
- ❏ Clown
- ❏ Coffeepot
- ❏ Comb
- ❏ Crown
- ❏ Elephant
- ❏ Fish
- ❏ Flashlight
- ❏ Flower
- ❏ Flying bats (10)
- ❏ Football
- ❏ Ghost
- ❏ Heart
- ❏ Hockey stick
- ❏ Hot dog
- ❏ Ice-cream cone
- ❏ Igloo
- ❏ Jack-o'-lantern
- ❏ Key
- ❏ Kite
- ❏ Mushroom
- ❏ Paintbrush
- ❏ Pencil
- ❏ Pizza
- ❏ Pyramid
- ❏ Sailor hat
- ❏ Top hat

This is the largest picture in the monster family album. It is the abominable snow kid building snow monsters. He has also thrown in some hidden pictures. Look closely to find them all.

- ❑ **Alligator**
- ❑ **Banana**
- ❑ **Bow tie**
- ❑ **Cactus**
- ❑ **Can**
- ❑ **Candle**
- ❑ **Cheese**
- ❑ **Chef's hat**
- ❑ **Cowboy hat**
- ❑ **Duck**
- ❑ **Fish**
- ❑ **Ghost**
- ❑ **Heart**
- ❑ **Hot dog**
- ❑ **Ice-cream cone**
- ❑ **Ice skate**
- ❑ **Ladder**
- ❑ **Lamp**
- ❑ **Lion**
- ❑ **Mouse**
- ❑ **Paintbrush**
- ❑ **Picture frame**
- ❑ **Pie**
- ❑ **Pig**
- ❑ **Pirate**
- ❑ **Shoe**
- ❑ **Shovel**
- ❑ **Top hat**
- ❑ **Umbrella**
- ❑ **Watering can**

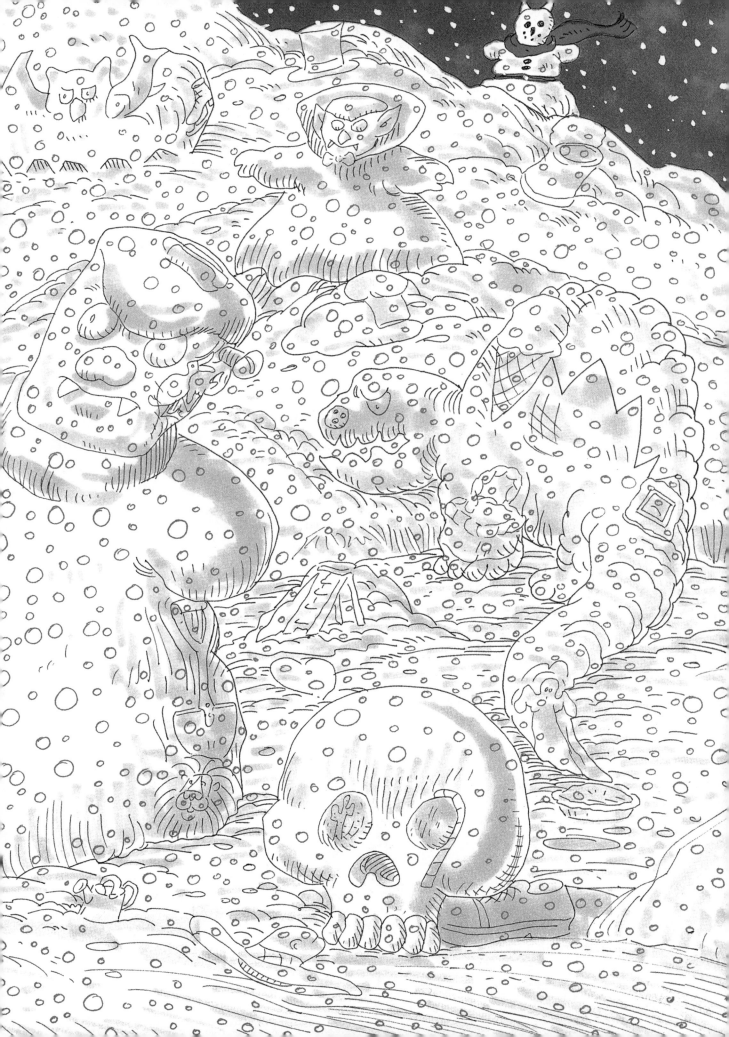

Here is the mummy, showing off his childhood pictures. You sure can get wrapped up in them! You also can get wrapped up in looking for the following hidden objects.

- ❏ Apple
- ❏ Arrow
- ❏ Artist
- ❏ Bird
- ❏ Blimp
- ❏ Bone
- ❏ Book
- ❏ Cupcake
- ❏ Drum

- ❏ Fish
- ❏ Football
- ❏ Ghost
- ❏ Golf club
- ❏ Hammer
- ❏ Kangaroo
- ❏ Kite

- ❏ Owl
- ❏ Pinocchio
- ❏ Sailor hat
- ❏ Saw
- ❏ Scarecrow
- ❏ Wagon

These are really terrific pictures—the best in the album! They are, of course, pictures of the invisible man throughout the years. Try to find the following objects:

- ❏ Banana
- ❏ Basket
- ❏ Bone
- ❏ Carrot
- ❏ Cheese
- ❏ Evergreen tree
- ❏ Fire hydrant
- ❏ Football
- ❏ Graduate's hat
- ❏ Guitar
- ❏ Hamburger
- ❏ Heart
- ❏ Hot dog
- ❏ Ice-cream soda
- ❏ Lightbulb
- ❏ Mouse
- ❏ Pear
- ❏ Pencil
- ❏ Rose
- ❏ Screwdriver
- ❏ Shovel
- ❏ Snail
- ❏ Star
- ❏ Television
- ❏ Tent
- ❏ Turtle
- ❏ Unicorn

FIRST BIRTHDAY ↵

KID LEAGUE STAR ↵

FIRST DAY OF SCHOOL ↵

INVISIBLE PAPER ↵

SCHOOL FIELD TRIP ↱

SOCCER CHAMP ↱

TALKING TO SANTA ↱

FIRST INVISIBLE MAN ON THE MOON ↱

One picture is too big to fit into the album.
It's so big, it's hiding the following hidden pictures:

- ❑ Balloons (2)
- ❑ Birdhouse
- ❑ Birds (2)
- ❑ Boat
- ❑ Clock
- ❑ Coffeepot
- ❑ Covered wagon
- ❑ Crown
- ❑ Dog
- ❑ Elephant
- ❑ Fish (3)
- ❑ Hearts (2)
- ❑ Horseshoe
- ❑ Jack-o'-lantern
- ❑ Key
- ❑ Kite
- ❑ Mailbox
- ❑ Mermaid
- ❑ Old radio
- ❑ Old sock
- ❑ Old tire
- ❑ Pizza
- ❑ Tepee
- ❑ Worm

The monsters are so happy to have shared their family album, they asked the children to pose with them for a group photograph. Before the picture can be taken, you must find the following objects:

- ❑ Bird's nest
- ❑ Bow tie
- ❑ Boxing glove
- ❑ Butterfly
- ❑ Camel
- ❑ Cow
- ❑ Crayon
- ❑ Dinosaur
- ❑ Eight ball
- ❑ Elephant
- ❑ False teeth

- ❑ Fish
- ❑ Flying bat
- ❑ Football
- ❑ Football helmet
- ❑ Hamburger
- ❑ Hammer
- ❑ Igloo
- ❑ Kite
- ❑ Locomotive
- ❑ Model plane
- ❑ Mouse

- ❑ Musical note
- ❑ Paintbrush
- ❑ Sled
- ❑ Snake
- ❑ Tent
- ❑ Thermometer
- ❑ Top hat
- ❑ Wind-up car

Early one morning, Frankie has a brilliant idea. He decides to visit some friends he hasn't seen in a long time.

FIND FRANKIE IN HIS NUTTY NEIGHBORHOOD, AND THESE FUN ITEMS:

- ❏ Book
- ❏ Bowling ball
- ❏ Bucket
- ❏ Candle
- ❏ Dog
- ❏ Duck
- ❏ Fish (3)
- ❏ Flying bats (3)
- ❏ Football helmet
- ❏ Hammer
- ❏ Heart
- ❏ Jack-o'-lantern
- ❏ Moose head
- ❏ Periscope
- ❏ Pinocchio
- ❏ Raincoat
- ❏ Roller skates
- ❏ Sailor hat
- ❏ Scarecrow
- ❏ Skier
- ❏ Skull
- ❏ Star
- ❏ Tepee
- ❏ Thermometer
- ❏ Tulip
- ❏ Turtle
- ❏ Watering can
- ❏ Wreath

Frankie first looks for his old, old friend Manny Mummy in a place with lots of sand.

FIND MANNY MUMMY IN THE DRY DESERT, AND THESE FUN ITEMS:

- ☐ Balloons (3)
- ☐ Banana peel
- ☐ Bathtub
- ☐ Birdhouse
- ☐ Brooms (2)
- ☐ Earring
- ☐ Fire hydrant
- ☐ Fish (2)
- ☐ Flower
- ☐ Gas pump
- ☐ Ring
- ☐ Sailor hat
- ☐ Sand castle
- ☐ Sand pail
- ☐ Sled
- ☐ Slingshot
- ☐ Snake
- ☐ Snowman
- ☐ Soccer ball
- ☐ Star
- ☐ Straw
- ☐ Suitcase
- ☐ Surfboard
- ☐ Turtle
- ☐ TV antenna
- ☐ Umbrella
- ☐ Watering can
- ☐ Watermelon slice

Frankie and Manny Mummy set off to find their friend Batty Bat. He lives in a strange place.

FIND BATTY BAT IN TERRIFYING TRANSYLVANIA, AND THESE FUN ITEMS:

- ❏ Alligator
- ❏ Arrows (2)
- ❏ Baker
- ❏ Bones (6)
- ❏ Book
- ❏ Bride and groom
- ❏ Broken heart
- ❏ Broken mirror
- ❏ Candle
- ❏ Dog
- ❏ Fish
- ❏ Flower
- ❏ Football
- ❏ Fortune teller
- ❏ Hair dryer
- ❏ Kite
- ❏ Lion
- ❏ Mouse
- ❏ Nail
- ❏ Octopus
- ❏ Rabbit
- ❏ Scissors
- ❏ Skulls (4)
- ❏ Top hat
- ❏ Training wheels
- ❏ Umbrella
- ❏ Vulture
- ❏ Worm

Now they are off to find another pal. This one lives in a swamp!

FIND SWAMPY SAM IN THIS MUSHY MARSH, AND THESE FUN ITEMS:

- ❑ Apple
- ❑ Cupcake
- ❑ Drum
- ❑ Football helmet
- ❑ Fork
- ❑ Frog
- ❑ Grand piano
- ❑ Hammer
- ❑ Key
- ❑ Lost boot
- ❑ Lost mitten
- ❑ Medal
- ❑ Moon face
- ❑ Necktie
- ❑ Palm tree
- ❑ Pencil
- ❑ Pizza slice
- ❑ Ring
- ❑ Snake
- ❑ Soccer ball
- ❑ Sock
- ❑ Speaker
- ❑ Spoon
- ❑ Toothbrush
- ❑ Trumpet
- ❑ Umbrellas (2)

Warren Werewolf is Frankie's next friend to find. He plays baseball with the Dead End Dodgers.

FIND WARREN WEREWOLF AT THE BALLPARK, AND THESE FUN ITEMS:

- ❏ Bicycle horn
- ❏ Bone
- ❏ Cactus
- ❏ Candy cane
- ❏ Carrot
- ❏ Cookie
- ❏ Crown
- ❏ Empty can
- ❏ Eyeglasses (2)
- ❏ Feather
- ❏ Fir tree
- ❏ Flamingo
- ❏ Footprint
- ❏ Frog
- ❏ Heart
- ❏ Horseshoe
- ❏ Humpty Dumpty
- ❏ Kite
- ❏ Lamp
- ❏ Pliers
- ❏ Six-fingered glove
- ❏ Skull
- ❏ Squirrel
- ❏ Tic-tac-toe
- ❏ Witch
- ❏ Worm

Frankie and his pals go to an old schoolhouse, where their friend Lena Lightning is a student.

FIND LENA LIGHTNING AMONG HER CREEPY CLASSMATES, AND THESE FUN ITEMS:

- ❏ Apple core
- ❏ Bell
- ❏ Bone tree
- ❏ Broken mirror
- ❏ Cactus
- ❏ Candles (3)
- ❏ Crystal ball
- ❏ Egg
- ❏ Firecracker
- ❏ Flashlight
- ❏ Flying bats (3)
- ❏ Fortune teller
- ❏ Hot dog
- ❏ Ice skate
- ❏ Mask
- ❏ Mouse
- ❏ Necktie
- ❏ Owl
- ❏ Pencil
- ❏ Saw
- ❏ Shark fin
- ❏ Skateboard
- ❏ Skunk
- ❏ Snakes (2)
- ❏ Star
- ❏ Vulture
- ❏ Worm

Next, Frankie and his friends set out to visit Greta Ghost, but none of her neighbors has seen her in a while.

FIND FRANKIE AND HIS OTHER FRIENDS AT GRETA'S HAUNTED HOUSE, AND THESE FUN ITEMS:

- ❏ Alligator
- ❏ Arrows (2)
- ❏ Axe
- ❏ Balloons (5)
- ❏ Banana peel
- ❏ Bowling ball
- ❏ Broom
- ❏ Cup
- ❏ Dart
- ❏ Drum
- ❏ Fork
- ❏ Hammer
- ❏ Hatched egg
- ❏ Heart
- ❏ Keys (2)
- ❏ Ring
- ❏ Screwdriver
- ❏ Ski
- ❏ Stool
- ❏ Sword
- ❏ Teapot
- ❏ Tepee
- ❏ Torn sock
- ❏ Turtle
- ❏ Umbrella
- ❏ Wreath

Frankie can't find Greta Ghost at the haunted house, so he and his friends check the new condos.

FIND GRETA GHOST IN MODERN MONSTERVILLE, AND THESE FUN ITEMS:

- ❑ Arrow
- ❑ Balloons (4)
- ❑ Bones (2)
- ❑ Camel
- ❑ Candles (3)
- ❑ Fire hydrant
- ❑ Fish (3)
- ❑ Flowers (3)
- ❑ Football helmet
- ❑ Frog
- ❑ Hoe
- ❑ Horseshoe
- ❑ Ice-cream cone
- ❑ Igloo
- ❑ Kites (2)
- ❑ Lollipop
- ❑ Lost bathing trunks
- ❑ Lost boot
- ❑ Mice (3)
- ❑ Painted egg
- ❑ Periscope
- ❑ Pyramid
- ❑ Quarter moon
- ❑ Rabbit
- ❑ Roller skates
- ❑ Sea horse
- ❑ Seal
- ❑ Sunglasses (2)

Together at last, the friends go on a picnic—where else but in a cemetery?

FIND FRANKIE AND HIS FRIENDS IN THIS GHOULISH GRAVEYARD, AND THESE FUN ITEMS:

- ☐ Apron
- ☐ Baseball cap
- ☐ Broom
- ☐ Bucket
- ☐ Burned-out candle
- ☐ Chef's hat
- ☐ Clothespin
- ☐ Crown
- ☐ Fish (2)
- ☐ Flower
- ☐ Guitar
- ☐ Heart
- ☐ House
- ☐ Lightbulb
- ☐ Mice (2)
- ☐ Paintbrush
- ☐ Picture frame
- ☐ Pig
- ☐ Ring
- ☐ Shovel
- ☐ Spoon
- ☐ Straw
- ☐ Tire
- ☐ Truck
- ☐ TV antenna
- ☐ Worm
- ☐ Wristwatch

After the picnic, Frankie and his friends go to see—you guessed it!—a monster movie.

FIND FRANKIE AND HIS FRIENDS AT THIS FRIGHTENING FLICK, AND THESE FUN ITEMS:

- ❑ Apple core
- ❑ Arrow
- ❑ Crown
- ❑ Dog
- ❑ Drum
- ❑ Eight ball
- ❑ Eyeglasses
- ❑ Faucet
- ❑ Fish skeleton
- ❑ Flashlight
- ❑ Fortune teller
- ❑ Heart
- ❑ Ice-cream pop
- ❑ Necktie
- ❑ Oilcan
- ❑ Paper airplane
- ❑ Periscope
- ❑ Piggy bank
- ❑ Rabbit
- ❑ Roller skates
- ❑ Sailboat
- ❑ Skunk
- ❑ Star
- ❑ Superhero
- ❑ Toast
- ❑ Top hat
- ❑ Trash can
- ❑ Trumpet
- ❑ Worm

While walking back from the movie, Frankie and his friends see a frightening sight!

FIND FRANKIE AND HIS FRIENDS WITH THESE TERRIFIC TRICK-OR-TREATERS, AND THESE FUN ITEMS:

- ❏ Balloon
- ❏ Broom
- ❏ Butterfly
- ❏ Candy cane
- ❏ Carrot
- ❏ Chef's hat
- ❏ Crown
- ❏ Earmuffs
- ❏ Fork
- ❏ Key
- ❏ Moustache
- ❏ Paintbrush
- ❏ Paper bag
- ❏ Pencil
- ❏ Pizza
- ❏ Roller skates
- ❏ Sailor hat
- ❏ Sock
- ❏ Star
- ❏ Top hat
- ❏ Tree ornament
- ❏ Umbrella
- ❏ Watering can
- ❏ Worm

$\mathcal{A}$T HOME WITH BREAD

Cooking Arts Collection™

CREDITS

About the Author

Lisa Golden Schroeder, founder of Foodesigns Culinary Consulting, learned her love for baking in a home filled with the scent of fresh bread. From winning her first county fair baking ribbons in high school, to teaching bread workshops and writing cookbooks with her mother, Ferol Smith Golden (who tested many of the recipes in this book), she has followed a path of good food and cooking throughout her 20 years in the food business. Her professional training includes a degree in nutrition and food science and journalism, and she holds an advanced diploma from La Varenne Ecole de Cuisine in Paris. A stint in the Betty Crocker Test Kitchens confirmed and refined her baking skills, which she still teaches to eager students. Lisa is a member of the International Association of Culinary Professionals and Les Dames d'Escoffier Internationale.

AT HOME WITH BREAD

Copyright © 2002 Cooking Club of America

Tom Carpenter, Director of Book Development
Jennifer Guinea, Book Development Coordinator
Greg Schwieters, Book Design and Production
Mark Macemon, Commissioned Photography
Lisa Golden Schroeder, Meg Brownson, Food Stylists

Special thanks to: Marcia Brinkley, Terry Casey, Elizabeth Gunderson, Bea Krinke, Pegi Lee, Nancy Mauer, Eric Melzer, Mary Jo Myers, Ruth Petran and Steve Schenten.

1 2 3 4 5 6 7 8 / 08 07 06 05 04 03 02
ISBN 1-58159-153-5

Cooking Club of America
12301 Whitewater Drive
Minnetonka, MN 55343
www.cookingclub.com

TABLE OF CONTENTS

"Every woman, high or low, ought to know how to make bread. If she does not, she is unworthy of trust and confidence, and, indeed, a mere burden upon the community."
— Cottage Economy, William Cobett, England, 1821

Oh how times have changed! Bread, once truly the staff of life, was such an important food source that it was a hanging offense to adulterate flour.

These days we can buy bread just about anywhere. Baking has become a luxury, a special pastime we can enjoy at home. Home-baked bread often becomes the highlight of celebrations and entertaining events. But because making bread is no longer an everyday chore, bakers need to become more at home with the process of working with water, flour and yeast. Mixing these building blocks, kneading dough, watching yeast work, knowing just when to pull the beautiful and aromatic loaves of bread from a warm oven … all are learned skills. These are the reasons we named this book *At Home with Bread* — because bread-baking is done at home, and because these pages de-mystify the process, truly making you at home with it.

Despite the accessibility of store- or bakery-bought breads — from the most pedestrian pre-sliced white pan loaves to rustic grainy artisan *boules* (balls) — nothing can compare to the yeasty aroma that wafts through the kitchen while fresh breads are baking in your own oven. You have the power to use any ingredients you like and do not have to compromise on quality or freshness. And the varieties are endless. Never let your baking become monotonous — try new recipes, new shapes and new flavors!

In our fast-paced culture, it's time to slow down and allow some time for the physical and spiritual release of creating a warm, crusty loaf. Many of my cooking students, some of them quite accomplished cooks, wistfully express their desire to learn to bake bread. The idea persists that bread-making is difficult, time-consuming and requires special knowledge to unlock its mysteries.

The following pages will reveal all the information you'll need to bake bread successfully, and also bestow the truth of baking — let the yeast do the work!

The majority of breads in this book are yeast-raised, requiring time for yeast organisms to do their work. Although time is essential, yeast doughs are very forgiving and their schedule can work around yours. They will still emerge beautiful and edible!

Sourdough breads, which have become a specialty style of baking, were once the only way that raised breads could be made. Capturing wild yeast spores from the air, these breads depend on interactions with good bacteria to create the organic reactions that make bread. There is wonderment to sourdough baking as you observe the yeast slowly bubbling away in the starter pot … and then again as you taste the amazingly different texture and flavor of the loaves you make.

Other breads offered here are considered "quick" breads — leavened with baking powder, soda, eggs or hot steamy air. Because of the speed in which their leavenings work, they tend to be less forgiving, but they also require less preparation and baking time. Some of the flatbreads (surviving the ancient history of baking outdoors over open fires by bakers that moved frequently with their herds or availability of food), require no leavening at all. They are simply tender doughs made from flour, water and salt.

It's time to be *At Home with Bread:* Creating delightful loaves in the comfort of your own kitchen, finding satisfaction and pleasure in the wonderful process, and sharing the extraordinary results with family, friends and guests.

BREAD ESSENTIALS

We all have kitchens equipped with what we need for cooking everyday meals. But a baker's kitchen requires a few essentials that you may not have on hand. The ingredients for baking bread are also different from what you may normally toss into your grocery cart. And the techniques and language associated with bread baking might be foreign to you. This primer will set the stage for launching you into the world of baking, making the process easy and enjoyable.

THE BAKER'S KITCHEN

Before you begin, take inventory of your kitchen shelves. There truly are only a few pieces of equipment that are a must, but there are several that you'll appreciate having around. Remember that the art of bread baking is extremely old. At one time, a lump of dough was just thrown into a fire to bake. So don't make the process any more complicated than necessary!

Accurate Ovens. Whether you have an electric or gas oven, it's good to know how accurate it is — many home ovens run 25 degrees hotter or cooler than the oven dial tells you. Place a mercury oven thermometer in the center of your cool oven, turn it on to 350°F and check the temperature in 15 minutes. If the oven is running higher or lower than 350°F, adjust accordingly when you're baking.

Large Mixing Bowls. Have at least two large-capacity bowls (6-quart or more) made of glass, ceramic or plastic. Mixing dough and allowing it to rise takes room. I prefer glass or ceramic bowls because they hold the dough's heat better, reducing rising time. Avoid metal for mixing doughs (especially sourdoughs), but smaller metal bowls are nice for mixing quick bread or muffin batters, making glazes, dissolving yeast and beating eggs.

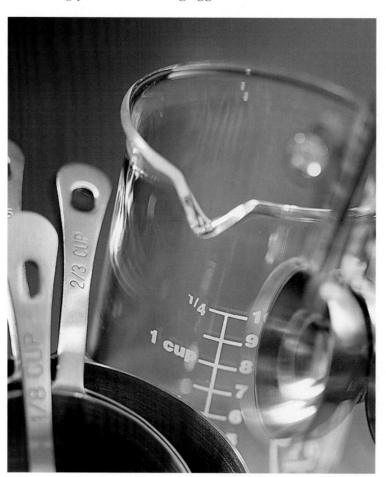

Measuring Equipment. At least one set of nested measuring cups, a 2-cup liquid measuring cup (glass or plastic) and measuring spoons are a must. Professional bakers actually weigh out all their ingredients to ensure accuracy and a consistent product. Most home bakers find it easier to use the standard kitchen measures they are familiar with.

Kitchen Timer. Use a timer to remind yourself to check on rising dough and keep tabs on bake times.

Instant Read Thermometer. This small temperature gauge on a probe is the easiest way to know if the liquids you use for yeast baking are warm enough to activate the yeast, but not so warm that they kill it.

Kitchen Towels, Plastic Wrap, Parchment Paper. I like to cover my doughs with a piece of plastic wrap and a clean kitchen towel while they're rising. Parchment paper is great for lining baking sheets — it eliminates pan scrubbing, and the parchment can be used over and over again.

Spoons, Rubber and Metal Spatulas, Pastry Scrapers. To stir up batters or doughs, large wooden, plastic or metal spoons are handy. Rubber spatulas (flexible rubber heads attached to a handle) work well to scrape batters or other soft mixtures into pans. Small metal spatulas are perfect for leveling off measuring cups. Pastry scrapers (free-form pieces of plastic in a half-moon shape or metal scrapers with a wood handle) can help with transferring and kneading soft doughs, and cleaning stubborn bits of dried dough off work surfaces.

Large Baking Sheets. Many free-form loaves, buns, rolls and coffee cakes need to bake on large, flat baking sheets. Use 16x12-inch flat aluminum sheets, with either shiny or nonstick finishes. Darker or black-coated baking sheets tend to bake very dark crusts; black carbon steel baking sheets can recreate the intense heat of a baking stone. Flat baking sheets are also good for sliding risen dough onto a baking stone in the oven.

Sharp Knives, Razor Blades, Lames, Shears, Pizza Wheels. Use a sharp knife (serrated ones work well) or razor blade to slash the tops of loaves. These slashes are both practical (allows gases that would otherwise tear the top crust to escape) and decorative. In Europe, a lame — a curved blade attached to a handle — is used for this purpose. Snip dough with kitchen shears to give a certain shape or personality to bread. A pizza wheel not only cuts baked pizza, but it also cuts rolled dough well.

Bread Pans. Rectangular loaf pans, either 8½x4½x2½ or 9x5x3 inches, are most common for American-style pan loaves. These pans also come in miniature sizes for gift-giving loaves. Look for medium weight metal, glass, ceramic or clay. Dark metal, again, will bake up thick, dark crusts. Glass pans require a lower baking temperature (25 degrees cooler than metal), but bake well and allow you to see browning crusts. Note that all the recipes in this book were tested in metal pans.

Other Baking Pans. Round or rectangular cake pans, rimmed jelly-roll pans, muffin tins, brioche molds, even pie plates and empty coffee cans can be used to mold breads. If you don't have the exact pan called for in a recipe, use what you do have, remembering that pans should be filled about one-half to two-thirds full before baking. A shallow roasting pan or 13x9-inch baking pan make good *bain-maries* (water baths) for creating steam in the oven. Because repeated usage as a water bath can discolor the inside of baking pans, you may want to use a heavy-duty aluminum foil pan or a retired pan.

Bannetons and Rising Baskets. In European bakeries, special baskets lined with canvas are called bannetons and used to rise the dough for round breads. The distinctive shape and design of these baskets gives an interesting look to breads. You can also line bowls or baskets with floured kitchen towels to give a more rustic look to your free-form loaves.

Rolling Pin and Pastry Brushes. Use a good rolling pin for shaping doughs both savory and sweet. My favorite is a long French pin with no handles, because there's nothing to get in the way of rolling large pieces of dough. A pastry brush is nice for glazing breads before and after baking.

Flour or Powdered Sugar Shaker. A metal or plastic canister with a fine wire-mesh top comes

in handy for dusting flour or sugar onto doughs or work surfaces.

Baking Stones. Ceramic stones, in rectangles or rounds, are available in many kitchen specialty shops for baking pizzas or breads. A stone can help recreate the baking environment of a stone hearth or wood-burning stove. Bake doughs either directly on the stone, in a pan or on a baking sheet. The heat from the stone makes the bread crustier. Before baking stones were commercially manufactured for the home baker, unglazed quarry tiles were sometimes used.

Pizza Peel or Paddle. In professional bakeries, a wooden paddle is traditionally used to slide bread onto a baking stone in the oven. Your dough can rise on the paddle or you can use a parchment or cornmeal-dusted baking sheet.

Spray Bottles. A standard household spray bottle or plant-mister filled with water helps create a steamy environment in the oven; this helps create crusty loaves.

Cooling Racks, Cutting Boards, Serrated Bread Knives. Wire cooling racks are essential baker's helpers for everything from bread to cakes. Baked goods need to cool with air circulating all around them, so the bottoms of loaves, muffins or rolls don't get soggy. Slicing bread on a cutting board protects countertops, tables and certainly your knives. Serrated knives cleanly slice soft bread without tearing it.

Handy Larger Kitchen Appliances. A standing electric mixer, food processor and yes, an electric bread machine, will all find uses in the baker's kitchen as well.

Stock your pantry with the following ingredients, the building blocks of bread baking, so you can bake at the drop of a hat.

THE GRANARY — FLOURS

Flour can be a tricky business. Depending on how fresh it is or how long (and where) it's stored, it can contain varying amounts of moisture. This is why most bread recipes call for a range of flour (for example, 3½ to 4 cups). You should begin by using the smallest amount, then add more as necessary.

The world of flour is huge, with more and more specialty flours becoming readily available. As you expand your baking repertoire, experiment with new grains to give even more flavor, texture and nutrition to your breads.

White Wheat Flour. This is the main flour used in breads because it has the highest amount of gluten protein. The germ and bran are stripped from the wheat endosperm before grinding, giving the flour a creamy white color. When mixed with liquid and kneaded or beaten, the gluten protein forms strands that stretch like elastic. These gluten strands create a structure that traps the bubbles of gas given off by the yeast activity, causing the dough to rise and expand into high, crusty loaves.

Hard spring and soft winter wheat varieties are ground into white flour, with hard red spring wheat being highest in protein and better for yeast-leavened breads.

All-Purpose Flour. This mixture of hard and soft wheat works well for certain yeast breads, quick breads and other baking. It works well in combination with higher gluten bread flour to make well-risen but still tender loaves.

Bread Flour. Depending on the baked good, too much gluten can be undesirable (like in cakes or biscuits), because you may want a very tender crumb and texture. Look for flour that is marketed as "bread" flour or any flour that has at least 16 grams protein per cup (most flour bags give nutrition info by the ¼ cup serving — so 4 grams protein per ¼ cup will give the 16 grams per cup). I call for unbleached wheat flours in these recipes, as I prefer to use organic flours when possible, and avoid those that have been chemically bleached.

Whole Wheat Flour. Milled from the entire wheat kernel, whole wheat flour retains the bran (outer hull) and germ (embryo or heart of the kernel). It's high in fiber and nutrients, but lower in gluten than white flour, so is often mixed with some white flour for better bread volume. Whole wheat flour is sometimes referred to as "stone-ground" if it's milled between two stones rather than modern metal rollers. This flour is usually available in fine and coarse grinds.

Graham Flour. This flour is basically whole wheat flour but is sometimes more finely milled. Whole wheat flour, like all whole grains, is more perishable because of its higher fat content from the germ. Store graham flour in a cool place (refrigerated or frozen in warm weather).

Semolina or Durum Flour. Ground from hard durum wheat, semolina is a pale golden yellow flour with a granular texture. Semolina is milled from the endosperm of durum wheat. It's usually used for making pasta but also makes good bread. Durum flour is ground from the whole durum wheat kernel or berry, and is a deep canary yellow.

Rye Flour. Available in light, medium or dark (also called pumpernickel flour or rye meal), rye is very low in gluten protein. It's almost always combined with some type of wheat flour in bread. It has a distinct fruity fragrance, and it makes a good base for sourdough starters because it ferments well.

Cornmeal. This finely ground flour from the dried kernels of sweet corn can also be found in medium to coarse grind (also known as soy grits or polenta). Cornmeal contains no gluten protein, so it's always combined with some wheat flour in yeast-leavened breads. Cornmeal also makes one of the most popular American quick breads, raised with baking soda or powder. Depending on the type you choose, cornmeal adds crunch and even color to breads. White, yellow, blue and even red cornmeal is available (blue and red Indian cornmeals are generally only found in the American southwest). You can sprinkle yellow cornmeal on baking sheets and stones to keep bread from sticking to the baking surface.

Buckwheat Flour. Buckwheat is milled from seeds which actually belong to the rhubarb family. Buckwheat imparts a unique flavor to breads and pancakes, and is made into noodles in Asia. Low in gluten protein, it is usually combined with wheat flour in a 1:3 ratio.

OTHER BAKING STAPLES

A home baker needs much more than just flour to create bread. Here are the other basics to have on-hand.

Baker's Yeast. Strains of this living single-celled organism are the miracles behind traditional yeast baking. Yeast feeds on flour and water and creates carbon dioxide (the gas that stretches the gluten strands), which makes dough rise. There are three types of commonly available commercial baking yeast: compressed cake (or fresh) yeast, active dry yeast and quick-rise yeast. I call for active dry yeast in all of the yeast-leavened breads in this book, but you can try substituting fresh or quick-rising yeasts to expand your baking experience.

Fresh Yeast Cakes. Cultivated from a different yeast strain than active dry yeast, yeast cakes activate more easily at cooler temperatures and have a milder flavor in baked products. Generally available in the dairy case, some grocers stock small 0.6-oz. cubes or larger 2-oz. cakes. One (0.6-oz.) cube of fresh yeast is equivalent to about 2¼ teaspoons (or one package) active dry yeast. When they have a high moisture content, yeast cakes can easily be crumbled and dissolved. Fresh yeast has a very short shelf-life — about two weeks refrigerated — so it's not the best option for occasional bakers.

Active Dry Yeast. Available as tiny brown granules, active dry yeast is sold in small ¼-oz. foil-wrapped packages or jars. Because bread machine yeast contains some stronger strains of baker's yeast and is more finely granulated, it dissolves more quickly than regular active dry yeast. One (¼-oz.) package of active dry yeast contains 2¼ teaspoons. It stores best in the refrigerator and can be stored one year, making it more convenient than fresh yeast for spur-of-the-moment baking.

Quick-Rise Yeast. This is another strain of a low-moisture granulated yeast that is similar to regular active dry yeast. Quick-rise yeast activates at a higher temperature. It is generally mixed with the flour and activated with very hot liquid, making the yeast act more quickly. Quick-rise yeast can cut a doughs' rise time nearly in half, and many recipes calling for this yeast have only a single rise time. But the flavor of your breads will suffer, as most breads benefit from slower, cooler, multiple risings. Yet if time is short, quick-rise yeast presents an alternative.

YEAST: WATCH THE DATES

It's important to make note of expiration dates on yeast packages. If the yeast has been stored properly you can be assured it will be alive and will work well in your baking. If your yeast is within its expiration date, there's no need to "proof" it; just activate it by dissolving it in warm liquid. If you're in doubt, dissolve the yeast in warm water with a pinch of sugar. If the yeast is alive, it will begin to bubble and foam within about 10 minutes.

Baking Powder and Soda. Both baking powder and soda are chemical leavening agents that also produce carbon dioxide gas when mixed with liquid and/or heat. Baking powder is double-acting, reacting to both liquids and heat. Baking soda, an alkaline substance, needs an acid to react. Many quick breads calling for baking soda also use buttermilk or molasses, both acidic ingredients.

Liquids. Liquids dissolve and activate yeast and other leavenings, and moisten flour so that the gluten strands can be developed. For yeast breads, a warm liquid is needed to awaken yeast organisms. Liquids should be warm to the touch, about 105°F to 115°F, but not too hot or the yeast will be killed. Water, milk, buttermilk, cream, fruit or vegetable juices, vegetable cooking water (like potato water), beer or broth can all be used.

MILK: STRATEGIES AND ALTERNATIVES

Milk is often used in American-style doughs, making them rise quickly, because yeast thrives on the natural lactose sugar in milk. Milk adds nice flavor and helps bread keep longer. Many years ago, before milk was pasteurized, it was necessary to "scald" milk (to heat just below the boiling point) in order to kill toxic microorganisms. Older baking recipes still call for scalding milk, but it's no longer necessary for food safety reasons. However, professional bakers have known for years that if large amounts of milk in a recipe are not scalded, there can be problems with the dough. "Slack" dough can be caused by a protein in milk that can inhibit yeast activity. I've found that in smaller amounts, this generally is not a problem for home bakers. All the recipes that call for milk in this book have been tested several times with no problems. The liquid milk is usually heated enough to activate the dry yeast. A convenient alternative to liquid milk is instant nonfat dry milk or dry buttermilk powder, which can be on-hand in your pantry.

Sweeteners. Granulated and brown sugars, honey, molasses and sorghum, barley malt syrup, fruit juices and maple syrup are many of the choices for sweet accents in breads. Yeast loves sweeteners, which can accelerate the speed of the yeasts' action. But sweeteners aren't necessary for the yeast to work, and are used primarily for their flavor and the textural and color influences they provide. Sweeteners help give bread a tender crumb and aid in the browning of crusts. Other liquids in recipes should be reduced a bit if liquid sweeteners, like honey or molasses, are used.

Salt. Salt is an important bread flavoring; without it, bread can taste flat and bland. Even sweet doughs benefit from a pinch of salt. It also works with the gluten to strengthen the structure of the bread, and helps control yeast activity. Many kinds of salt are available, from the most common iodized table salt to kosher (coarse) and sea salts. I prefer to use a granulated sea salt, primarily because of the flavor it imparts.

Fats. Not all breads contain fats. French baguettes, for instance, are made only of flour, water, yeast and salt. These breads are wonderful freshly baked, but become stale very quickly. Butter or margarine, oils and shortenings are common fats used in breads, contributing to flavor, moisture and a soft golden crust — and giving them staying power. Breads with fat can last up to one week before becoming stale. I prefer to use butter and oils (olive oil in particular because of its superior taste) in my baking. In certain recipes, sour cream, yogurt, half-and-half or cream can add fat.

Eggs. Eggs add richness, color and texture (in both strength and tenderness) to breads. Many doughs rely on eggs as an essential ingredient. Examples include brioche dough and other breakfast-style breads. When baking, be sure to only use large eggs. Using smaller (or larger) eggs can negatively affect the volume and texture of baked goods.

Specialty Ingredients. Seeds, whole grains, nuts, dried fruits, herbs and spices all add variety and new dimensions to your baking. Look for multi-grain cereals,

rolled oats, cracked or bulgur wheat, bran flakes, rye or wheat flakes and wheat germ to stir into doughs. Cooked whole grains like wheat berries, brown or wild rice or barley can add moisture, texture and a hefty dose of fiber and nutrition. Sesame, poppy, caraway and other seeds boost flavor in a big way, along with sunflower seeds and toasted nuts. Flax seeds add valuable nutrition. Raisins, currants, dried cranberries, apricots, dates and figs are sweet, chewy and colorful. And grated citrus peel imparts an incomparable freshness to any bread.

Many ingredients benefit from special handling, making them the perfect final touch for adding to dough: a dash of toasted nuts or spices, a sprinkling of stripped dried fruit, or a dollop of tender cooked whole grains. Just stir into the dough as you create it.

Toasting Nuts

Toasting nuts deepens their flavor, and they are crisper when toasted too.

Place nuts in an ungreased baking pan and toast in a 350°F oven 8 to 10 minutes, stirring occasionally, until golden brown and fragrant. Or place nuts in a dry skillet and cook over medium heat 5 to 7 minutes, stirring or shaking the pan frequently, until the nuts are golden brown.

To toast and remove the slightly bitter skin from hazelnuts, toast them in the oven 10 minutes or until golden brown and the skins crack and blister. Wrap the hazelnuts in a clean kitchen towel and rub them around until most of the dark skin comes off (it's fine if some of the skin remains on the nuts).

Toasting Seeds

Cumin, sesame and caraway seeds are especially delicious if they have been toasted. Here's how. Place seeds in a dry skillet over medium heat. Cook and stir 3 minutes or until just golden and very fragrant. Remove seeds immediately from the skillet or they will continue to cook.

Cutting Dried Fruit

Place sticky dried fruit, such as apricots, dates or prunes, on a cutting surface and dust with a little flour. Use a chef's knife to chop the fruit into small pieces. Or use kitchen shears sprayed with nonstick cooking spray to snip the fruit into pieces.

Cooking Whole Grains

Wild rice, brown rice, pearled barley, wheat berries or rye berries all require about one hour to cook and become very tender so they become great stir-ins for breads.

The general proportion of liquid to grain is a 2:1 ratio. Bring liquid and grains to a boil in a heavy saucepan; reduce heat to low, cover and simmer 45 to 60 minutes or until the grains are very tender and have burst. The liquid should be completely absorbed. Let the grains cool before using.

This can be done ahead and the grain kept refrigerated. Depending on the bread, I sometimes use broth or apple juice instead of water to cook grains. Add some spices, herbs or chopped garlic for more flavor.

Hydrating Other Grains

Some cracked or flaked grains (wheat, oats, rye, barley or cornmeal) and multi-grain hot cereals are better if they are hydrated (soaked) in hot water, or cooked briefly, before being added to doughs. Most recipes give directions for doing this if needed.

$\mathcal{T}$HE BAKER'S TECHNIQUES

There are two basic kinds of yeast dough — batter and kneaded. Batter breads are really short-cut, no-knead yeast breads, and rely on strong beating either by hand or machine to develop the gluten structure. Kneading requires more energy, and a willingness to get your hands into the flour and dough. Both types need time for the yeast to work.

TO BEGIN

Measure ingredients carefully when baking. Flour needs accurate measuring to ensure that doughs will be the right texture. Spoon flour into a dry measuring cup, then level off with a straight-edged spatula or a knife. Use glass or plastic measuring cups for liquids, reading the measurement at eye level.

Activating yeast is usually the first step to making bread doughs. Because yeast likes a warm environment to grow, it needs to be awakened with warm liquid. Yeast is usually dissolved in liquid that is between 105°F and 115°F. If you use fresh yeast, the liquid should be a little cooler, closer to 95°F. Use an instant read thermometer to make this a foolproof step, because if the liquid is hotter than 115°F the yeast will die. Once the yeast is dissolved, the fermentation process begins, and you can begin mixing in the rest of the dough ingredients.

When mixing dough for **batter breads,** less flour is used and the dough is stickier. The first addition of flour is either vigorously beaten in by hand or with an electric mixer. Spread the batter into the pan and allow it to rise once. These breads have a coarser texture and a pebbled surface.

For **kneaded breads,** there are two ways of mixing the dough: the sponge method and the straight mixing method.

The **sponge method** allows for the yeast to be dissolved in a liquid, then mixed with only part of the flour. This batter is allowed to stand anywhere from 30 minutes to overnight. Standing allows the yeast to work longer and develop a tangy flavor before stirring in the remaining flour and other ingredients that make the bread. This method makes a slightly more compact, moist loaf that's good for slicing for sandwiches. Because the flour is given more time to absorb the liquid, you won't need quite as much flour as a straight mixed dough.

The **straight mixing** method is just that — the yeast is dissolved in part of the liquid, then the rest of the ingredients are added as soon as the yeast dissolves. The dough is kneaded right away and allowed to rise before shaping and baking.

KNEADING

Once most of the ingredients have been mixed in, it's time to **knead** the dough. This can be done by hand, in a heavy-duty electric mixer fitted with a dough hook, in a food processor, or in a bread machine.

The process consists of vigorously pushing, pulling and working the ingredients into a smooth and elastic ball, using the heels of your hands on a work surface. Doing this develops the gluten strands that will give structure to the bread.

KNEADING: INSIDE SECRETS

What does elastic mean? The dough should feel lively and bouncy — or as my great-grandmother would say, "soft as a baby's bottom." The key to success with breads is to learn what the dough should feel like, and this takes practice. Remember this old country adage: Don't worry the dough; work it thoroughly but thoughtfully, but don't pummel it.

The weather can have an effect on the amount of extra flour required as you knead dough. If it's hot and humid you can expect your dough to be stickier and require a bit more flour. But be cautious — dust your work surface or dough with just enough flour to prevent sticking (this is where a shaker with a wire-mesh top comes in handy — just shake a little flour onto your work surface). If you knead in too much extra flour, your dough will feel heavy and when baked it will be dry. The goal is to keep your dough as moist as you can while still being able to work with it. Often, flavoring ingredients like nuts or fruits are kneaded in at the end of the process, or even after the first rising, so they don't become smashed or broken up.

EASIER KNEADING

If you prefer to keep your hands out of the dough, here are a few ways to ease the kneading process.

Use a Large Electric Standing Mixer with Dough Hook. Follow the recipe as directed, mixing ingredients in a mixer bowl. Mix in the minimum amount of flour called for, making a stiff but moist dough. Beat dough at high speed until smooth and elastic, about 8 to 10 minutes. If the dough sticks to the side of the bowl or feels sticky to the touch, add a bit more flour until it pulls free or no longer feels sticky. Leave dough in the bowl to rise.

Use a Large Capacity (at Least 8-Cup) Food Processor. Follow the recipe as directed, mixing the ingredients in the food processor bowl with the plastic dough blade or a metal blade. Mix in the minimum amount of flour called for and process until the dough forms a ball and pulls from the container side. Process about 45 seconds longer. If the dough feels sticky, add 1 tablespoon flour at a time; blend with short bursts. Remove the dough to a greased bowl to rise.

Use an Electric Bread Machine (Using Dough Cycle). Load room temperature bread ingredients into the bread machine pan (at least 1½-lb. loaf capacity) according to the manufacturer's directions. Select Dough cycle; press Start. When the cycle is finished, remove the dough and shape as directed in the recipe. Let rise once more before baking. *(Note that doughs made in a bread machine tend to be very soft and may need to be kneaded with a little more flour before shaping.)*

RISING DOUGH

Standard Rising. Once the dough is smooth and elastic, it's time to allow the yeast to go to work. Put the dough back into a large bowl that will give it plenty of room to expand. I like to use the original mixing bowl — why use more bowls than necessary? Clean it out with hot water and lightly grease the inside to keep the dough from sticking. By turning the dough over after placing it in the bowl, the top will not dry out or stick to whatever is covering it during rising.

Alternative Method. Another method of rising is to dust the top of the dough with flour. Loosely cover the bowl — I like to use a sheet of plastic wrap, then a clean kitchen towel — and place it in a warm place (preferably about 80°F). Let the dough stand until it has expanded to twice its size, or some recipes say "doubled in bulk." This generally takes about 1 to 1½ hours. The temperature of the rising environment depends on the style of baking you use: Longer, cooler rises help develop the flavor of the dough, while others are fine with room temperature rises. Some doughs, especially ones made with whole grains or lower gluten flours, just need more time to rise.

RISING DOUGH: SOME TIME FOR FLEXIBILITY

Make the dough work around your schedule. If you are going to be gone, it's okay to let the dough rise for as long as you need it to — or if you're not ready to shape it when it's doubled, gently deflate it and allow it to rise again. You can do this up to four times with a single dough.

Cool Rising. Another method of letting dough rise is referred to as "cool rising." Place the dough in the refrigerator, covered with plastic wrap, for several hours or up to overnight. The cool temperature slows the yeast's action, so the dough rises more slowly and actually develops more flavor.

Preparing Dough for Shaping. Generally, what you look for once you're ready to shape the dough is a dramatic increase in size, and a light and spongy structure. When you press two fingers into the dough the indentations don't spring back.

Punching Dough. The usual terminology for what to do next runs the gamut from "punching" or "knocking" down the dough to "gently deflating" it. Here's how:

• Uncover the dough and press into it firmly with your hands or fists, but not violently. This expels large gas bubbles and refines the texture of the dough.

• Turn the dough out onto a floured surface and you're ready to shape it as your recipe suggests, or as creatively as you wish.

SHAPING DOUGH

There are infinite ways to shape dough, from traditional pan loaves and braids to European baguettes shaped like wheat sheaves to pretzels to dinner rolls.

Standard Loaves. The easiest way to form an even, beautifully-domed pan loaf is to roll the dough out into a rectangle (about 18x9-inches) with a rolling pin. Roll it up jelly-roll fashion from the short side, sealing the seam and ends well. Place dough into a greased loaf pan.

Baguettes. To form French baguettes, follow the same procedure as above but roll the dough from the long side, seal the seam and place on cornmeal-dusted baking sheets. Make diagonal slashes along the top of baguettes. Loaves can be shaped into large rounds or oblongs with tapered ends.

Braided Loaves. Braided loaves can be free-form or baked in loaf pans, but the procedure is the same: Divide the dough into three even pieces. Roll each piece into a long rope. Lay the ropes side by side on your work surface, overlapping them in the center. Braid the ropes from the center to both ends, sealing well. You can begin braiding from the top of the ropes, but the braid may not be as even.

Preparing for Proofing. Once the dough is shaped, place it into greased pans or on a greased or parchment-lined baking sheet. Some recipes call for dusting baking sheets with cornmeal or other coarse grain to prevent sticking and to add texture to the bread crust. You may also decide to make decorative slashes on top of your dough at this point, or brush it with beaten egg white or spritz with water to attach a sprinkling of seeds or grains. This may also be done just before baking, depending on the look you desire. Cover the dough with plastic wrap or drape it loosely with a slightly damp kitchen towel.

PROOFING (THE SECOND RISE)

Your shaped dough now needs to rest and be allowed to rise, or proof, once more before baking. This second rise is usually shorter than the first one and it's important not to overproof or the dough can collapse in the oven or fill with large air pockets. This rising is a delicate time and should happen in a warm place away from cool drafts of air. The dough should nearly double again in size, or appear puffy and feel spongy when pressed gently.

To delay baking, refrigerate shaped dough and let it proof slowly in the cool air (part of the cool rising method mentioned before). This is a good technique for entertaining, as you can hold shaped dinner rolls or other favorite bread until just before your guests arrive. They can then be greeted with the aroma of freshly baked bread as they sit down to the table.

DUSTING, SLASHING AND SNIPPING

Just before baking there are many ways to enhance the appearance and flavor of breads. For a rustic look, spray dough with a little water and dust it with flour. For a shinier and glazed look, brush the dough with beaten egg white or whole egg. Or sprinkle the dough with seeds, toasted spices or nuts for extra crunch.

Slashing or snipping the dough with kitchen shears can give new shape to dough (snipping into the tops of rolls will create interesting peaks). Slashing dough provides an attractive design and also allows the bread to expand more in the oven without splitting the crust or becoming unevenly shaped. Slash dough firmly and decisively with a single-edged razor blade or sharp serrated knife. If the dough is sticky, flour the knife blade. Make the cuts at 45-degree angles on the diagonal for a traditional look. Try a checkerboard pattern or create your own signature design!

INTO THE OVEN

Preheat your oven at least 15 to 20 minutes before you are ready to bake, so that the heat will be evenly distributed. It is a good idea to double-check the accuracy of your oven thermostat periodically with a mercury oven thermometer.

Baking Stones. You may choose to use a ceramic baking stone to imitate a professional baker's stone-lined oven. A stone provides even heat distribution under your breads and helps create crisp, chewy crusts. I prefer to place my stone on the lowest rack in my oven, but many bakers place it in the center of the oven. The most important thing is to have good air circulation around the stone so that your bread will bake evenly.

Place your stone in the oven before preheating and be sure it has at least 20 minutes to heat. Breads can be slid directly onto the stone; dust it with cornmeal before heating to prevent dough from sticking, or use a wooden pizza paddle with cornmeal under the dough. Rolls or other smaller baked goods can be baked on a baking sheet directly on a stone.

Adding Humidity. To recreate the humid environment or steam used in professional ovens, you can spritz the inside walls of your oven with water from a spray bottle. Quickly spray water just before placing the dough inside, then several times more during the first minutes of baking.

Other methods for making steam include tossing a handful of ice cubes inside a foil pie pan placed in the bottom of the oven; steam will rise up as the ice melts. Or place a 13x9-inch baking pan or shallow roasting pan, half-filled with hot water, in the bottom of the oven. The easiest way to do this is to place the pan in the oven during the preheating period. Steam will be released in the oven until the pan is removed; remove the pan after the first 20 minutes of baking so that the crust begins browning.

HIGH ALTITUDE CONSIDERATIONS FOR BAKING

Slight adjustments need to be considered when baking at a high altitude (3,500 feet or higher).

Yeast Breads. Yeast breads tend to rise more quickly at higher altitudes where the air is thinner and the atmospheric pressure is lower. Doughs may be drier, as well. To adjust for a higher altitude, you may need to:

- reduce the amount of yeast in recipes by ½ teaspoon.
- add up to ¼ cup more liquid.
- be careful of the amount of flour you knead into doughs and add a bit more salt (up to ¼ teaspoon) to help control or slow yeast activity. Rise times may need to be shortened a bit, as well.

Quick Breads. Quick breads (those leavened with baking powder or soda, especially breads and cookies) generally require little adjustment. However, some recipes might need an increased oven temperature (an additional 25°F), increased liquid, a little less leavening and possibly less sugar or a larger pan size.

DETERMINING DONENESS

In the first 10 minutes of baking, the dough will have a final burst of gas expansion, called "oven spring." At this point the yeast dies as the internal temperature of the bread rises above 140°F. The crust begins to form, and the heat begins to set the gluten structure.

Browning Insights. Follow the suggested baking times offered in recipes, but look for crust brownness as a clue to when the bread is close to being done. Sometimes breads, especially those with a lot of sugar, begin to brown too quickly as the sugar in the dough begins to caramelize. If browning occurs too early during baking, lay a sheet of foil over the overbrowned area or the entire loaf. This deflects heat from the crust while allowing the bread to finish baking.

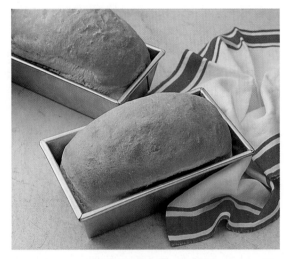

How to Check Doneness. Check a loaf's doneness by tapping the crust with a fingertip or removing the pan from the oven and tapping the bottom. It should sound hollow. If it doesn't, return it to the oven five to 10 minutes longer. Learn to trust your senses as you smell the bread baking and see it brown. And listen for that hollow sound that indicates the inside is no longer doughy.

Correct Cooling. Cool breads in pans or on baking sheets for at least 10 minutes before removing them to a wire cooling rack. Yeast breads should cool at least 30 minutes before slicing (although tearing into a warm French baguette is sometimes irresistible) to allow their internal structure to solidify and any excess moisture to evaporate.

Slicing. Serrated bread knives are designed for slicing bread without tearing or mashing the bread. Slice bread with a sawing motion. To slice pan loaves easily and evenly, place them on a cutting board lying on their side.

STORING BREAD

Store bread wrapped in either a plastic bag or foil; be sure it's completely cool before wrapping. Most breads are best eaten within a few days, if stored in a cool dry place. If it is hot and humid outside, the refrigerator can be a good storage option; the cool air slows mold growth. Breads made with milk, butter and eggs will last longer than those without, and whole grain and rye breads are especially good keepers.

Home-baked breads are one of the nicest things to keep in the freezer. If stored properly, they will taste nearly as fresh as when they were first made when thawed or reheated. Wrap bread well in plastic, then seal securely in foil. Make sure you label each item and include the date.

THAWING BREAD

To thaw frozen bread, let it stand in its wrapping at room temperature for two to three hours. Or unwrap frozen bread, brush away any ice crystals and rewrap in foil. Place in a 350°F oven 20 to 30 minutes. If the crust should be crisp, reheat the loaf unwrapped on a baking sheet.

Wrap individual frozen rolls — like bagels, pretzels or dinner rolls — in a paper towel or waxed paper and microwave *just* 20 to 30 seconds or until thawed and warm.

ABOUT QUICK BREADS

What makes them quick? Quick breads are leavened by baking powder, baking soda, eggs or hot steam — rising agents that require little time to work compared to yeast-leavened breads. Batter quick breads include sweet loaves, muffins, popovers and cornbreads. Dough quick breads include biscuits, scones and soda breads.

QUICK BREAD INGREDIENTS

Flour. Wheat flour is the basis for quick breads. But because these breads are quickly prepared and their structure doesn't require gluten development, they're best made with all-purpose flour. The crumb of quick breads should be tender, not tough, so flour ground from soft as well as hard wheat is preferable.

Baking Powder and Soda. Both baking powder and baking soda are chemical leavenings that work quickly when mixed with liquid and heat.

Baking powder was introduced in 1856, and changed the face of American baking by giving home bakers much more

predictable results. The double-acting baking powder available today is a mixture of acid and alkaline ingredients. It comes in airtight cans and needs to be replaced regularly to ensure good baking results. Baking soda, a natural alkaline originally known as *saleratus*, was the first chemical leavening known in the U.S. It needs to be paired with an acidic ingredient (buttermilk, sour milk, molasses, honey, chocolate, etc.) to create the carbon dioxide bubbles that will raise baked goods.

Eggs. Eggs strengthen and enrich quick breads. In the case of popovers, eggs become a leavener. Oven heat solidifies the protein in eggs, which produces steam that causes batters to rise.

Fats. Many quick breads — especially denser-crumbed ones like tea breads or muffins — include fats like oil, butter or shortening. In older recipes for cornbreads or biscuits it was common to see lard or bacon fat used. Fats make an important contribution to the flavor and texture (dense or flaky) of many quick breads.

QUICK BREAD METHODS

Few words are needed to explain the best methods for making quick breads. The most critical advice is that both quick bread batters and doughs should be handled quickly and gently. In fact the less handling, the better the bread.

Handling Batters. Quickly stir the wet ingredients into the dry ingredients, just until they are moistened — the batter should still be a little lumpy.

Handling Dough. The fat used should be chilled and cut into the dry ingredients like you do when making pastry dough. Mix the liquid in swiftly, then gently knead the dough on a floured surface, just enough to pull the dough together. Overkneading results in a tough, rather than tender, bread.

QUICK BREAD NOTES

- Loaf pans, cake pans, baking sheets and muffin tins are essential equipment.
- To test doneness during baking, check breads with a wooden pick inserted in the center. A golden-brown crust is the best doneness test for dough-type breads.
- Cool tea loaves completely before slicing; you can serve muffins, biscuits and cornbread warm.
- Most quick breads last for several days at room temperature, and freeze beautifully for longer storage.

SOURDOUGH: NOTES AND TECHNIQUES

An important category of kneaded yeast bread is **sourdough baking**. A sourdough starter is based on a yeast-and-bacteria culture that ferments for long periods at room temperature. This style of leavening results in breads that have a rich, deep and often acidic (or sour) flavor. These breads have thick, chewy crusts and long shelf lives.

The sourness of a starter depends on the length of time it is allowed to ferment and the ingredients used. The starter is the leavening base that the rest of the bread ingredients are mixed and kneaded with. After rising, the dough is baked like other yeast breads. Using the starter as the only leavening in a bread requires longer rise times. Sometimes additional yeast is added but is not necessary. Baking methods that incorporate steam only enhance the already naturally thick crusts of these breads.

In this book, you'll find water- and milk-based batter-style starters that can be kept alive indefinitely in the refrigerator if fed and cared for on a regular basis. There is also a more dough-like starter based on the European pre-ferment tradition that uses a bit of commercial yeast. It is like an Italian *biga*, which takes less time to make — about a day before baking — compared to the French *chef*, that takes many days to ferment. With the biga, you make it fresh each time you plan to bake. The flavor it imparts is mildly sour, and the bread is dense, moist and keeps well. The French chef starter has a more sour flavor, and a part of the dough from one batch of bread (called the *levain*) is saved to start the leavening of subsequent bread batches. This is similar to the style used in classic San Francisco sourdough breads.

MASTER DOUGHS

In this chapter, you'll find tried and true "master dough" recipes — basic doughs that can be used in other recipes in this book. As you master these doughs, you will develop the confidence to tackle any scratch baking recipe. And you can use any of these doughs as a starting point for inventing your own signature breads — and practice braiding, twisting, rolling and layering dough with fillings.

Perfect White Bread Dough, page 32

NRICHED EGG DOUGH

Adding more eggs and butter to bread dough makes it richer in flavor, and particularly good for making special dinner rolls or breads and holiday indulgences for entertaining.

1 (¼-oz.) pkg. active dry yeast	¾ cup sugar
¼ cup warm water (105°F to 115°F)	5 to 5½ cups unbleached all-purpose flour
¾ cup butter or margarine, cut into chunks	1 large egg yolk beaten with 1 tablespoon water
⅓ cup milk	
5 eggs	

❶ In large bowl, dissolve yeast in water; let stand 5 minutes. In small saucepan or microwave, heat butter and milk until milk is just warm (110°F — butter does not need to melt).

❷ Add milk mixture, eggs, sugar and 2 cups of the flour to yeast mixture; beat until smooth. Stir in 3 cups flour; beating until soft, somewhat sticky dough forms.

❸ Scrape dough onto floured surface; dust lightly with flour. Knead until very smooth and elastic, adding just enough remaining flour to keep dough from sticking, at least 10 to 15 minutes. Place in greased bowl; turn dough greased side up. Cover; let rise in warm place 1½ to 2 hours or until doubled in size.

❹ Punch dough down; turn out onto lightly floured surface. Knead briefly. Shape as directed in desired recipe or freeze dough.

❺ To bake dough, shape as desired. Cover; let rise 30 to 45 minutes or until puffy. Brush with egg yolk mixture. Bake in 350°F oven 25 minutes or until golden brown.

18 servings.
Preparation time: 3 hours, 10 minutes.
Ready to serve: 3 hours, 35 minutes.
Per serving: 255 calories, 10 g total fat (5.5 g saturated fat), 90 mg cholesterol, 70 mg sodium, 1 g fiber.

VARIATION   Spiced Egg Dough
Add 1 teaspoon ground cinnamon, ½ teaspoon ground ginger and ¼ teaspoon ground nutmeg in step 2.

100% HONEY WHOLE WHEAT DOUGH

Dense and moist, this hearty dough makes loaves or rolls that are a joy to eat — even the kids will love them! And of course, whole wheat breads provide more vitamins, minerals and fiber than white breads.

1½ cups water	½ cup honey
1½ cups milk	2 teaspoons salt
1 (¼-oz.) pkg. active dry yeast	6¾ to 7¾ cups fine stone-ground whole wheat flour
3 tablespoons light olive oil or melted butter	

❶ In small saucepan or microwave, heat water and milk until just warm (110°F). Pour into large bowl. Dissolve yeast in warm liquid; let stand 5 minutes. Add oil, honey, salt and 3 cups of the flour. Beat vigorously with wooden spoon or mixer 2 minutes. Add enough remaining flour (about 3½ cups) to create manageable dough.

❷ Turn dough out onto lightly floured surface. Knead 8 to 10 minutes or until smooth and elastic. Place in greased bowl; turn greased side up. Cover; let rise in warm place 1½ to 2 hours or until doubled in size.

❸ Punch dough down. Use as directed in desired recipes or divide in half and freeze in resealable plastic freezer bags.

❹ To make loaves, grease 2 (9x5-inch) loaf pans. Divide dough in half; shape into loaves and place in pans. Cover; let rise in warm place 30 to 45 minutes or until nearly doubled in size. Heat oven to 350°F. Bake 35 to 40 minutes or until golden brown.

24 servings.
Preparation time: 3 hours, 10 minutes.
Ready to serve: 3 hours, 55 minutes.

Per serving: 160 calories, 2.5 g total fat (0.5 g saturated fat), 1 mg cholesterol, 205 mg sodium, 4 g fiber.

BAKER'S NOTES

• Because whole wheat flour maintains the germ and bran of the wheat kernel, this dough requires more kneading to develop the gluten structure in the bread (but don't go too far, as the sharp edges of the bran will begin to cut the newly developed gluten strands).

• A longer rising time gives a lighter texture and more wheaty flavor.

ERFECT WHITE BREAD DOUGH

This is adapted from my grandmother's favorite recipe for everyday bread.

1 (¼-oz.) pkg. active dry yeast	⅓ cup nonfat dry milk
3 cups warm water (105°F to 115°F)	2 teaspoons salt
3 tablespoons sugar	¼ cup butter or lard, softened, plus additional for brushing loaves
⅛ teaspoon ground ginger	
6½ to 7 cups unbleached bread flour	

❶ To make sponge: In small bowl, dissolve yeast in ½ cup of the water. Stir in ½ teaspoon of the sugar and ginger; let stand 10 minutes. In large bowl, combine remaining sugar, 1 cup water, 2 cups of the flour and dry milk, mixing well. Stir in yeast mixture. Cover bowl; let stand 1 hour, until sponge is well risen and bubbly. Stir 1½ cups water, salt and ¼ cup butter into sponge; beat well. Stir in 4 cups flour, mixing until manageable dough forms that clears sides of bowl.

❷ Turn dough out onto floured surface. Knead dough 8 to 10 minutes or until smooth and elastic, using as much remaining flour as needed to prevent sticking. Place in greased bowl; turn dough greased side up. Cover; let rise in warm place 1 hour or until doubled in size. Punch dough down. Use as directed in desired recipes or divide in half and freeze in resealable plastic freezer bags.

❸ To make loaves, grease 2 (9x5-inch) loaf pans. Punch dough down; turn out onto lightly floured surface. Knead 2 minutes; divide dough in half. Shape into 2 loaves; place in pans. Brush tops of loaves with softened butter. Cover; let rise 45 minutes or until nearly doubled in size. Heat oven to 350°F. Bake 40 minutes or until golden brown. Remove loaves from pans; cool on wire rack.

24 servings.

Preparation time: 3 hours, 35 minutes.

Ready to serve: 4 hours, 15 minutes.

Per serving: 165 calories, 2.5 g total fat (1.5 g saturated fat), 5 mg cholesterol, 215 mg sodium, 1 g fiber.

AYBREAK MUFFIN MIX

Keep this mix on hand for quickly fixing a batch of morning muffins, even on the busiest of days.

4½ cups unbleached all-purpose flour	1 cup packed dark brown sugar
4 cups oat bran	3 tablespoons baking powder
3 cups multigrain oatmeal (mixture of rolled rye, barley, oats and wheat) or old-fashioned rolled oats	2 tablespoons grated orange peel
	1 tablespoon salt
1½ cups nonfat dry milk or dried buttermilk	2 teaspoons apple pie spice

❶ Mix flour, oat bran, oatmeal, dry milk, sugar, baking powder, orange peel, salt and apple pie spice in large covered container or jumbo plastic resealable bag. Store airtight at room temperature up to 6 months.

48 servings.

Preparation time: 15 minutes.

Ready to serve: 20 minutes.

Per serving: 115 calories, 1 g total fat (0 g saturated fat), 0 mg cholesterol, 250 mg sodium, 2 g fiber.

ISQ-EASE BISCUIT STARTER

Stirring up your own mix is less expensive and allows you to use nutritious whole wheat flour.

6 cups unbleached all-purpose flour	⅔ cup nonfat dry milk
2 cups whole wheat flour	4 teaspoons salt
¼ cup baking powder	1 cup butter, shortening or lard

❶ In large bowl, combine all-purpose flour, whole wheat flour, baking powder, dry milk and salt; mix well. Cut in butter with pastry blender or 2 knives until mixture has a fine, even crumb. Place mix into large plastic resealable bag or covered container. Store airtight in refrigerator no longer than 3 months.

40 servings.

Preparation time: 15 minutes.

Ready to serve: 20 minutes.

Per serving: 135 calories, 5 g total fat (3 g saturated fat), 13 mg cholesterol, 415 mg sodium, 1 g fiber.

# AYBREAK MUFFINS

Filled with whole grain cereals, all this mix needs is water, egg, oil and your choice of fresh or dried fruit and nuts — a nutritious meal in a muffin!

3 cups *Daybreak Muffin Mix* (page 34)

1 cup water

¼ cup vegetable oil

1 egg

½ cup fresh blueberries, chopped apple, chopped banana, raisins or snipped dried plums (prunes) or apricots

¼ cup chopped walnuts, pecans, hazelnuts or sunflower seeds, if desired

❶ Heat oven to 400°F. Grease bottoms only of 12 medium muffin cups, or line with paper baking cups. In medium bowl, combine muffin mix, water, oil and egg; mix just until dry ingredients are moistened (batter will be lumpy). Stir in fruit and nuts.

❷ Spoon batter evenly into muffin cups. Bake 16 to 18 minutes or until golden brown around edges (tops will be a pale golden color). Remove muffins from cups and serve warm.

12 servings.

Preparation time: 10 minutes.

Ready to serve: 30 minutes.

Per serving: 190 calories, 7.5 g total fat (1 g saturated fat), 20 mg cholesterol, 260 mg sodium, 2.5 g fiber.

VARIATION Texas-Size or Gem Muffins

Spoon prepared batter into 6 jumbo muffin cups or 24 mini muffin cups. Bake jumbo muffins about 20 minutes and mini muffins 12 to 15 minutes.

BAKER'S NOTES

• Be sure your baking powder is fresh, so you know that each batch of muffins will rise well. Check the bottom of the baking powder can for a freshness or expiration date.

• Don't have apple pie spice on hand? For 2 teaspoons, mix 1 teaspoon ground cinnamon, ½ teaspoon ground nutmeg, ¼ teaspoon allspice and ¼ teaspoon ground cloves or ginger.

ISQ-EASE BISCUITS

Biscuits are probably one of America's most popular quick breads, found in many convenience forms from refrigerated dough to dry baking mixes. The best, of course, are those made from scratch, hot and fragrant from the oven.

2½   cups *Bisq-Ease Biscuit Starter* (page 34)
¾   cup water

❶ Heat oven to 450°F. In medium bowl, combine biscuit starter and water; mix until dry ingredients are moistened. Turn out onto lightly floured surface. Gently knead dough 8 to 10 times.

❷ Pat dough out to ½-inch thickness. Using 2½- to 3-inch round cutter, stamp out 10 to 12 biscuits.

❸ Place biscuits on baking sheet. Bake 12 to 15 minutes or until golden brown.

10 servings.
Preparation time: 5 minutes.
Ready to serve: 17 minutes.
Per serving: 135 calories, 5 g total fat (3 g saturated fat), 15 mg cholesterol, 415 mg sodium, 1 g fiber.

VARIATION   Cheesy Spiral Biscuits

Prepare biscuit dough as directed. Roll out dough into ¼-inch-thick rectangle. Sprinkle with ½ cup shredded cheddar cheese or other preferred cheese. Roll up; cut into ½-inch slices. Place on baking sheet and bake until golden brown, or bake on top of casseroles.

BAKER'S NOTES

• Biscuits should rise to about twice their original height (about 1-inch thick when baked), with a light, fluffy interior and a golden brown crust.

• The dough should be gently kneaded just until smooth. This develops the gluten just enough to give the dough an extra push in the oven without making the biscuits tough or chewy.

• Use lightly floured pastry cloth when kneading, rolling and cutting out biscuits. The cloth makes re-rolling the dough easier and eliminates the need to use more flour to keep dough from sticking.

$\mathcal{S}$WEET YEAST DOUGH

This dough is easy to handle and rises quickly.

2 (¼-oz.) pkg. active dry yeast
1¼ cups warm water (105°F to 115°F)
⅓ cup granulated or packed brown
   sugar
⅓ cup nonfat dry milk
1 teaspoon salt

⅓ cup butter or margarine,
   softened
2 eggs
5½ to 6 cups unbleached all-purpose
   flour

❶ In large bowl, dissolve yeast in ½ cup of the water; let stand 5 minutes. Stir in remaining ¾ cup water, sugar, dry milk and salt. Beat in butter, eggs and 2½ cups of the flour until well blended. Stir in 2½ cups flour; beat until smooth. Add enough remaining flour to create manageable dough.

❷ Turn dough out onto lightly floured surface. Knead 8 to 10 minutes or until dough is smooth and elastic. Place in greased bowl; turn dough greased side up. Cover; let rise in warm place 1 hour or until doubled in size.

❸ Punch down dough. Turn out onto lightly floured surface and shape as directed in desired recipe. Let rise; bake as directed.

24 servings.
Preparation time: 2 hours.
Ready to serve: 2 hours, 30 minutes.
Per serving: 155 calories, 3.5 g total fat (2 g saturated fat), 25 mg cholesterol, 125 mg sodium, 1 g fiber.

BAKER'S NOTES

- If a dough is risen to twice its size before you're ready to use it, you can punch it down and let it rise again, or refrigerate it until you're ready to shape it.
- This dough is stickier than *Perfect White Bread Dough*. Using a floured pastry cloth or lightly oiling your hands before kneading will make handling the dough easier.

COMPLEMENTS: SPREADS AND DIPS

INDIAN SPICED HONEY

1	cup wildflower honey
1	teaspoon grated fresh ginger
1	teaspoon ground cinnamon
½	teaspoon ground cloves or allspice

❶ Place honey, ginger, cinnamon and cloves or allspice in small saucepan over medium heat. Simmer, stirring frequently, 5 minutes. Remove from heat. Let stand 10 minutes.

❷ Pour honey into clean jar or squeeze bottle. Refrigerate up to 3 months. Serve on warm toast, with fresh fry bread or warm over waffles or pancakes.

❸ To make a variation known as *Warm Orange Cardamon Honey*, substitute 2½ teaspoons ground cardamon and 1 teaspoon grated orange peel for the ginger, cinnamon and cloves or allspice.

1 cup.

CREAM CHEESE SPREAD

1	(3-oz.) pkg. cream cheese, softened
2	tablespoons prepared basil pesto
¼	cup powdered sugar
½	cup softened butter or margarine
1	tablespoon grated orange or lemon peel

❶ In a food processor or blender, process cream cheese, pesto, sugar, butter and grated orange until smooth. Refrigerate. Serve with bread or breadsticks. Store refrigerated for up to 4 days

½ to 1 cup.

ROASTED RED PEPPER SPREAD

1	large red bell pepper, roasted and peeled or 1 cup jarred roasted bell peppers
¼	cup firmly packed fresh basil
2	garlic cloves, minced
1	tablespoon balsamic vinegar
2	teaspoons extra-virgin olive oil

❶ In food processor or blender, process bell pepper, basil, garlic, vinegar and oil until smooth. Pour into medium saucepan; bring to a boil. Stir over medium-high heat 3 minutes or until thickened. Cool. Serve with bread or breadsticks. Store refrigerated up to 4 days.

½ cup.

PERFECT WHITE DOUGH BREAD WITH INDIAN SPICED HONEY

AROMATIC DIPPING OILS

It's easy to make your own gourmet dipping oils, at a fraction of the cost of store-bought imports. Note that these oils should be refrigerated and kept no longer than two to three weeks, due to the risk of anaerobic bacterial growth. Because olive oil will harden in the refrigerator, remove from refrigerator about 30 minutes before using to bring to room temperature.

ROSEMARY ORANGE OIL

    2   medium oranges

    1   cup extra-virgin olive oil

    1   cup fresh rosemary (stripped from stems), rinsed, drained

❶ Grate zest (the colored part) from oranges, using a citrus zester, microplane grater or small holes on box grater. In small saucepan, combine orange zest, oil and rosemary leaves. Gently warm mixture over low heat 6 minutes until fragrant. Process mixture in blender or food processor 25 seconds or until herbs are chopped. Pour into very clean glass measuring cup; cover and refrigerate at least 24 hours or up to 48 hours.

❷ Line funnel with cheesecloth. Pour Rosemary Orange Oil into funnel; let drip into very clean jar or bottle (this takes time). Cover or cork tightly and label with date. Store refrigerated up to 3 weeks.

12 servings.

Preparation time: 1 hour, 45 minutes.

Ready to serve: 25 hours, 45 minutes.

Per serving: 120 calories, 13.5 g total fat (2 g saturated fat), 0 mg cholesterol, 0 mg sodium, 0 g fiber.

VARIATION   Garlic Chive Lemon Oil

Substitute ½ cups chopped garlic chives for the rosemary and zest of 1 lemon for the oranges.

FINISHING TOUCHES

Here are some tips and techniques for making all your loaves interesting and perfect.

CRUST TREATMENTS

To make the crust you want, follow these guidelines.

- **To create a softer crust on a loaf.** Spread softened or melted butter or margarine over shaped dough before baking, or brush onto crust of warm loaves after baking.
- **For a drier, crustier finish.** Brush tops of loaves with water before baking, or dust loaves with flour, cornmeal or other grains.
- **For a clear, shiny finish.** Cook a mixture of 1 teaspoon cornstarch and ½ cup water over medium heat 1 minute. Brush onto baked loaves just as they finish baking. Return loaves to oven and bake 2 to 3 minutes longer.

EGG WASHES OR GLAZES

Brush one of the following mixtures onto bread dough just before baking, to create beautifully browned and/or glossy crusts.

- Whole egg beaten with 1 tablespoon water: Glossy crust; aids browning.
- Whole egg beaten with some water and honey: Glossy crust; aids browning.
- Whole egg beaten with 1 tablespoon milk: Glossy crust; aids browning.
- Egg white beaten with 1 tablespoon water: Glossy crust; good for attaching seeds, chopped nuts or dry seasonings to dough.
- Egg yolk beaten with 1 tablespoon water: Aids browning.

BASIC POWDERED SUGAR GLAZES

These glazes will liven up any bread.

VANILLA, ALMOND, RUM OR COCONUT GLAZE

1 cup powdered sugar

3 to 5 teaspoons milk, juice or other liquid (orange, lemon, lime or apple juice or maple syrup)

¼ to ½ teaspoon flavoring extract (vanilla, almond, rum, coconut, etc.), if desired OR 2 teaspoons grated citrus peel (orange, lemon, lime) if desired

❶ Combine all ingredients in small bowl, mixing until smooth and of desired consistency. Drizzle over cooled baked goods or spread over warm ones for a more translucent glaze.

HONEY GLAZE

½ cup honey

¼ cup butter or margarine

❶ Warm honey and butter together until butter is melted. Brush over warm baked goods.

JAM OR JELLY GLAZE

¼ cup fruit jam or jelly (apricot, marmalade, currant, etc.)

❶ Gently warm jam (sieve out large chunks of fruit) or jelly until melted. Brush onto warm baked goods, such as breakfast breads or Danish.

THE AFTERMATH

Follow these guidelines for making croutons and bread crumbs from leftover or stale bread.

- **Plain Toasted Croutons.** Heat oven to 350°F. Remove crusts from thick slices of bread. Slice bread into ½-inch strips, then crosswise into ½-inch cubes. Spread in a single layer on baking sheet. Bake 10 to 15 minutes, turning once or twice, until lightly toasted; cool. These freeze well. Use in salads and bread stuffings, or on top of casseroles.
- **Garlic ´n Herb Croutons.** Prepare bread cubes as above. Toss bread with some olive oil, chopped garlic and desired dried herbs. Bake as directed above; cool.
- **Dry Bread Crumbs.** Place day-old or stale bread in food processor; process until fine crumbs are formed. Spread in even layer on baking sheet. Dry at room temperature, covered with a paper towel, or lightly toast in 350°F oven. Cool; use immediately or freeze.

WHITE LOAVES

Think about Grandma's towering domed loaves, with a creamy crumb and hint of sweetness, sporting a beautiful golden crown. Imagine a crisp and crusty French baguette — warm and satisfying in every way. You really can create bread this good. Here's how. It doesn't get better than this!

French Baguette (Pain Ordinaire), page 54

$\mathcal{I}$TALIAN MARKET BREAD

This staple bread is enriched with a little olive oil, but is very similar in composition to a classic French bread. However, by starting with a sponge that can stand up to 12 hours, the flavor of the bread develops more and the texture is finer, with fewer holes.

2	(¼-oz.)pkg. active dry yeast	1½	teaspoons salt
2	tablespoons sugar	2	tablespoons olive oil
2½	cups warm water (105°F to 115°F)	1	egg white beaten with 2
6 to 7	cups unbleached all-purpose flour		tablespoons water

❶ In large bowl, dissolve yeast and sugar in water; let stand 5 minutes. Stir in 3 cups of the flour; cover and let sponge stand at least 30 minutes or up to 12 hours; sponge should be bubbly and risen.

❷ Add salt and oil to sponge. Beat in 2 cups flour until stiff dough forms. Turn dough out onto surface spread with 1 cup flour. Knead 10 minutes or until very smooth and elastic, adding remaining flour as needed to prevent sticking. Place in greased bowl; turn dough greased side up. Cover; let rise in warm place 1 hour or until doubled in size.

❸ Punch dough down; divide in half. Sprinkle large baking sheet with cornmeal. On floured surface, shape each half into loaf 15-inches long and about 5-inches wide. Place on baking sheet. With sharp serrated knife or razor blade, make diagonal slashes across tops. Cover; let rise 45 minutes or until nearly doubled in size.

❹ Heat oven to 350°F. Place 13x9-inch pan half-filled with boiling water on bottom rack or floor of oven. Brush dough with egg white mixture and bake in center of oven 45 to 50 minutes or until golden brown. Slide pan of hot water out of oven after first 20 minutes of baking.

24 servings.
Preparation time: 3 hours, 10 minutes.
Ready to serve: 4 hours.
Per serving: 130 calories, 1.5 g total fat (0 g saturated fat), 0 mg cholesterol, 150 mg sodium, 1 g fiber.

VARIATION Seeded Italian Bread

Before baking, brush with egg white mixture. Sprinkle loaves with sesame seeds, celery seeds or poppy seeds as desired.

OREGON HERB BREAD

This curved, luxuriant loaf celebrates the wonderful bounty of fresh summer herbs available in the temperate climate of the Pacific Northwest.

1	(¼-oz.) pkg. active dry yeast	2	teaspoons chopped fresh sage or ½ teaspoon dried
2	tablespoons sugar	1½	teaspoons onion or garlic salt
1¼	cups warm water (105°F to 115°F)	½	teaspoon freshly ground pepper
3½ to 4	cups unbleached bread flour	½	cup butter, softened
½	cup wheat germ	1	egg
¼	cup nonfat dry milk		Cornmeal
1	tablespoon chopped fresh dillweed or 1 teaspoon dried	1	tablespoon butter, melted
2	teaspoons chopped fresh tarragon or ½ teaspoon dried		

❶ In large bowl, dissolve yeast and sugar in water. Let stand 5 minutes. Stir in 1½ cups of the flour, wheat germ, dry milk, dillweed, tarragon, sage, onion salt and pepper. Beat in softened butter, egg and enough remaining flour to make soft dough.

❷ Turn dough out onto lightly floured surface. Knead dough 6 to 8 minutes or until smooth and elastic. Place in greased bowl; turn dough greased side up. Cover; let rise in warm place 1 hour or until doubled in size. Sprinkle large baking sheet with cornmeal. Punch dough down; turn out onto lightly floured surface. Shape into log, 24- to 26-inches long. Twist log into a figure 8; pinch ends together. Place on baking sheet. Cover; let rise 45 minutes or until nearly doubled in size.

❸ Heat oven to 375°F. Bake 25 to 35 minutes or until deep golden brown, tenting with foil during last 10 minutes to prevent excess browning. Brush top of loaf with melted butter; sprinkle with additional herbs, if desired. Cool on wire rack.

16 servings.
Preparation time: 2 hours, 15 minutes.
Ready to serve: 2 hours, 45 minutes.
Per serving: 170 calories, 4.5 g total fat (2.5 g saturated fat), 25 mg cholesterol, 185 mg sodium, 1.5 g fiber.

VARIATION Oregon Orchard Bread

Omit onion salt and herbs; use 1 teaspoon regular salt. Knead in ⅓ cup chopped toasted hazelnuts and ⅓ cup snipped pitted dried plums (prunes) during last few minutes of kneading.

CRACKED PEPPER CHEESE BREAD

A better party bread can't be found! This very large, lush braid is filled with peppery richness. Sliced diagonally, it pairs well with fresh ripe pears and makes wonderful sandwiches with smoked meats, watercress and tart chutney.

1 (¼-oz.) pkg. active dry yeast	2 eggs
1¾ cups warm water (105°F to 115°F)	1 teaspoon freshly ground pepper or pepper mélange (mixture of different colored peppercorns)
2 tablespoons sugar	
5½ to 6½ cups unbleached all-purpose flour	1 cup (4 oz.) shredded sharp cheddar cheese
⅓ cup nonfat dry milk	1 egg yolk beaten with 1 tablespoon water
2 tablespoons softened butter	
1 teaspoon salt	

❶ In small bowl, dissolve yeast in ½ cup of the water. In large bowl, combine remaining 1¼ cups water, sugar, 2 cups of the flour and dry milk. Beat in yeast mixture. Add butter, salt, eggs, pepper and enough remaining flour; stir until manageable dough forms.

❷ Turn dough out onto floured surface. Knead 8 to 10 minutes, adding more flour as needed to form smooth and elastic dough. Flatten dough with hands, sprinkle ¼ cup of the cheese over surface. Roll dough up and flatten again. Repeat process until all the cheese is worked into dough. Knead lightly to be sure cheese is evenly distributed through dough. Place in greased bowl; turn dough greased side up. Cover; let rise in warm place 1 hour or until doubled in size.

❸ Grease large baking sheet. Punch dough down; turn out onto lightly floured surface. Divide into 3 equal pieces; roll into 28-inch ropes that are tapered at each end. Lay strips on baking sheet. Starting in middle, braid strips to each end, tucking ends under and pressing each end down lightly to pan. Cover; let rise 1 hour or until nearly doubled in size.

❹ Heat oven to 350°F. Brush dough with egg yolk mixture. Bake 30 to 35 minutes or until golden brown (tent with foil if crust begins to brown too quickly). Cool on wire rack.

24 servings.
Preparation time: 2 hours, 40 minutes.
Ready to serve: 3 hours, 15 minutes.
Per serving: 150 calories, 3.5 g total fat (2 g saturated fat), 35 mg cholesterol, 145 mg sodium, 1 g fiber.

OVERNIGHT AMISH POTATO BREAD

This recipe uses the by-products of cooked potatoes (potato water and mashed potatoes) in bread dough! This practice was very popular in the nineteenth and twentieth centuries in Europe and the U.S.

1	(¼-oz.) pkg. active dry yeast	2	eggs
2	tablespoons sugar or molasses	2	cups mashed potatoes
1½	cups warm potato water (105°F to 115°F)	6 to 7	cups unbleached all-purpose flour
1	tablespoon salt		

❶ In large bowl, dissolve yeast and sugar in potato water. Stir in salt, eggs and mashed potatoes. Stir in flour, 1 cup at a time, beating well after each addition, until very stiff dough forms (about 5 cups).

❷ Turn dough out onto floured surface. Knead 10 to 12 minutes, adding enough remaining flour until dough is smooth and very elastic. Shape into a ball; place in greased bowl, turning greased side up. Cover tightly; refrigerate overnight to rise (up to 16 to 18 hours). If you want to bake the same day: Let dough rise in warm place 1½ hours or until doubled in size.

❸ Grease 2 (9x5-inch) loaf pans. Punch dough down; divide in half. Form 2 loaves and place in pans. Cover; let rise 2 to 3 hours or until doubled in size (if dough was refrigerated; if baking the same day this takes only about 45 minutes).

❹ Heat oven to 375°F. Dust tops of loaves with flour; bake 30 to 35 minutes or until golden brown. Remove loaves from pans; cool completely on wire racks.

24 servings.
Preparation time: 19 hours, 50 minutes.
Ready to serve: 20 hours, 20 minutes.
Per serving: 145 calories, 1.5 g total fat (0.5 g saturated fat), 20 mg cholesterol, 330 mg sodium, 1 g fiber.

VARIATION Rich Dilled Potato Bread
Substitute ½ cup milk for ½ cup of the potato water, and add ¼ cup softened butter and 1 tablespoon dill seeds to dough in Step 1.

BAKER'S NOTES
- For potato water and mashed potato: Simmer 2 medium russet potatoes until very tender. Reserve 1½ cups of the cooking water, allowing it to cool while you peel and mash the potatoes.
- The long, cool rise of the dough not only develops flavor in the bread, but also allows for flexibility in baking time.
- This bread's moist texture comes from the potato. It makes great toast and keeps well refrigerated.

$\mathcal{L}$ACED SPINACH-RICOTTA BREAD

Stromboli, calzone, pasties or meat pies — whatever the name, these savory filled breads and pastries makes great portable lunches or snacks. The bread machine short-cuts the dough-making process, and the filling variations are endless. Lacing the dough over the spinach and cheese makes the bread look more interesting and is no more difficult than just folding the dough over a filling.

3 cups unbleached bread flour	1 cup low-fat ricotta cheese
1 cup lukewarm water	2 egg yolks
2 tablespoons olive oil	½ cup (2 oz.) freshly grated Parmesan cheese
1 (¼-oz.) pkg. active dry yeast or 2¼ teaspoons bread machine yeast	¼ teaspoon freshly grated nutmeg
6 garlic cloves, minced	Cornmeal
½ teaspoon salt	1 cup (4 oz.) shredded smoked Provolone
1 (10-oz.) pkg. frozen chopped spinach, thawed, squeezed dry	1 egg, beaten

❶ Place flour, water, oil, yeast, garlic and salt into 1½-lb. loaf bread machine, following manufacturer's instructions. Select Dough cycle; press Start.

❷ Prepare filling: In medium bowl, mix spinach, ricotta, egg yolks, Parmesan and nutmeg. Turn dough out of bread pan onto floured surface. Knead 30 seconds until smooth; cover and let rest 10 minutes. Sprinkle large baking sheet with cornmeal.

❸ Roll dough into 15x10-inch rectangle. Spread filling lengthwise over center third of dough. Sprinkle Provolone over filling. With sharp knife, make cuts from filling to edges of dough at 1-inch intervals along sides. Alternating sides, fold strips at an angle across filling. Use foil or parchment paper to transfer filled dough to baking sheet. Cover; let rise in warm place 45 minutes or until nearly doubled in size.

❹ Heat oven to 350°F. Brush dough with beaten egg; bake 35 minutes or until golden brown. Cool slightly before slicing.

16 servings.
Preparation time: 3 hours, 15 minutes.
Ready to serve: 3 hours, 55 minutes.
Per serving: 190 calories, 7 g total fat (3 g saturated fat), 50 mg cholesterol, 235 mg sodium, 1 g fiber.

VARIATION Ham and Cheese Dijon Sandwhich
Add 3 tablespoons Dijon mustard to dough. Prepare dough and roll out as directed. Layer 1 cup chopped smoked ham and ½ cup cubed Swiss cheese down center of dough. Lace up as directed.

TAOS PUEBLO BREAD

This bread has its roots in the southwestern U.S., where ground corn is not only a main ingredient in tortillas, but finds its way into many types of baked breads.

1½ tablespoons active dry yeast	¾ cup whole wheat flour
2 tablespoons honey or molasses	1 teaspoon salt
1¼ cups warm water (105°F to 115°F)	1 cup stone-ground yellow or white cornmeal, plus additional for dusting loaf
2 tablespoons vegetable or olive oil	
1½ to 2 cups unbleached bread flour	

❶ In small bowl, dissolve yeast and honey in water. Let stand 5 minutes. Stir in oil.

❷ In large heavy-duty food processor fitted with plastic dough blade (or use metal blade if you don't have dough blade), combine 1½ cups of the bread flour, whole wheat flour and salt; process 30 seconds to mix. With motor running, pour in yeast mixture. Process until smooth, scraping work bowl down as needed.

❸ Add 1 cup cornmeal; process until soft mass of dough gathers together and begins to clear sides of work bowl (it will be soft and sticky). Add more bread flour, up to ½ cup, as needed to form soft dough that is not excessively sticky. Process about 30 seconds to knead.

❹ Turn dough out into greased bowl. Cover; let rise in warm place 1½ to 2 hours or until doubled in size.

❺ Grease 9x5-inch loaf pan. Punch dough down; turn out onto lightly floured surface. Shape dough into loaf and place in pan; dust with cornmeal. Cover; let rise in warm place 1 hour or until nearly doubled in size. Heat oven to 375°F. With sharp serrated knife or razor blade, make 4 diagonal slashes across top of loaf. Lightly spritz or brush with water; dust with cornmeal. Bake 25 to 30 minutes or until light golden brown. Remove from pan; cool on wire rack.

16 servings.

Preparation time: 3 hours.

Ready to serve: 3 hours, 30 minutes.

Per serving: 125 calories, 2 g total fat (0.5 g saturated fat), 0 mg cholesterol, 145 mg sodium, 2 g fiber.

VARIATION Desert Sage Cornmeal Bread

Add 2 teaspoons crumbled dried sage to flour mixture in food processor. Bake as large free-form loaf on cornmeal-dusted baking sheet. Slash top of loaf as directed, but brush lightly with beaten egg white and sprinkle with chopped hulled pumpkin seeds.

PAIN DE CAMPAGNE

A country-style French loaf with herbs, this free-standing round loaf has a slashed top crust that's dusty with flour.

1 cup each water, milk
½ cup chopped red onions
2 teaspoons dried *herbes de Provence* or 1 teaspoon dried rosemary, crushed
3 tablespoons olive oil
2 tablespoons sugar
1½ teaspoons salt

¾ teaspoon freshly ground pepper
1 (¼-oz.) pkg. active dry yeast
½ cup rye flour
3½ to 4½ cups unbleached all-purpose flour, plus additional for dusting loaves
Cornmeal

❶ In medium saucepan over medium heat, combine water, milk, onion, herbs, oil, sugar, salt, and pepper. Heat until warm (105°F to 115°F). Pour water mixture into large bowl. Sprinkle in yeast to dissolve. Stir in rye flour and 1 cup of the all-purpose flour; beat until smooth. Stir in enough remaining flour to make dough easy to handle.

❷ Turn dough out onto lightly floured surface. Knead 6 minutes or until smooth and elastic. Place in greased bowl; turn dough greased side up. Cover; let rise in warm place 1 hour or until doubled in size. Punch down dough. Turn out onto lightly floured surface; divide in half. Let rest 10 minutes. Shape each half into tight 5-inch round loaf. Place loaves on large baking sheet sprinkled with cornmeal. Cover; let rise 45 minutes or until doubled in size.

❸ Heat oven to 375°F, with baking stone on lowest oven rack, if desired. With sharp serrated knife or razor blade, make 3 diagonal slashes (½-inch deep) across top of each loaf; make 3 additional diagonal slashes in opposite direction. Dust with flour. Just before putting loaves in oven, spritz inside of oven with water. Slide loaves onto baking stone or bake on baking sheet. Bake 20 to 25 minutes or until golden brown. Cool on wire rack.

16 servings.
Preparation time: 2 hours, 30 minutes.
Ready to serve: 3 hours.
Per serving: 155 calories, 3 g total fat (0.5 g saturated fat), 0 mg cholesterol, 225 mg sodium, 1.5 g fiber.

BAKER'S NOTES
- *Herbes de Provence* is a distinctive blend of dried herbs from southern France. The mixture usually includes rosemary, thyme, tarragon, basil, savory, cracked fennel seeds, lavender and marjoram.
- Depending on the size of your baking stone and bread, you may need to bake one loaf at a time. If so, refrigerate the second loaf to slow the rising process while the first loaf bakes. Bake the second loaf just a few minutes longer.

GOLDEN SEMOLINA SESAME RING

An Italian country classic, this ring loaf is made entirely of semolina flour from the hard durum wheat that is also used to make pasta.

1	tablespoon active dry yeast	3½ to 4	cups semolina flour
1½	cups warm water (105°F to 115°F)	1	egg white beaten with 1 tablespoon water
1	teaspoon toasted sesame oil		Cornmeal
2	tablespoons nonfat dry milk		
1	teaspoon salt		
¼	cup toasted unhulled or hulled sesame seeds		

❶ In large bowl, dissolve yeast in ½ cup of the water; let stand 5 minutes. Stir in remaining 1 cup water, sesame oil, dry milk and salt. Stir in 2 tablespoons of the sesame seeds and 3 cups of the semolina, beating with wooden spoon or electric mixer until soft, very sticky dough forms.

❷ Turn dough out onto surface dusted with ¾ cup semolina. Knead dough 8 to 10 minutes, adding semolina as needed to prevent sticking, until dough is smooth and elastic. Place in greased bowl; turn dough greased side up. Cover; let rise in warm place 1½ or 2 hours or until doubled in size.

❸ Sprinkle large baking sheet with cornmeal; set aside. Punch dough down. Turn out onto semolina-dusted surface. Roll dough into 18x12-inch rectangle. Roll up tightly jelly-roll fashion, starting from long side. Pinch seam to seal well. Lay roll on baking sheet, pulling ends together to form a ring. Cover; let rise 45 to 50 minutes or until nearly doubled in size.

❹ Heat oven to 350°F. Brush dough with egg white mixture; sprinkle with remaining 2 tablespoons sesame seeds. Bake 30 to 40 minutes or until light golden brown. Cool on wire rack.

16 servings.
Preparation time: 3 hours.
Ready to serve: 3 hours, 40 minutes.
Per serving: 130 calories, 1.5 g total fat (0.5 g saturated fat), 0 mg cholesterol, 155 mg sodium, 1 g fiber.

VARIATION   Tunisian Bread

Add ½ teaspoon anise seeds with sesame seeds in Step 1.

BAKER'S NOTES

• To toast sesame seeds, place hulled or unhulled seeds in a dry skillet. Cook over medium heat, stirring frequently, 2 to 3 minutes or until golden brown and very fragrant. Be sure to remove seeds from the pan immediately, because they'll continue to toast in the hot pan and can burn easily.

# FRENCH BAGUETTES (PAIN ORDINAIRE)

This is classic, crusty bread. Eat it the day it's made!

1 tablespoon active dry yeast
2¾ cups warm water (105°F to 115°F)
1 tablespoon salt

6 to 7 cups unbleached all-purpose or bread flour
1 egg beaten with 1 tablespoon milk, if desired

❶ In large bowl, dissolve yeast in 1 cup of the water; let stand 5 minutes. Stir in remaining 1¾ cups water, salt and 5½ cups of the flour until soft dough forms. Turn dough out onto heavily floured surface. Scrape dough up and over into flour with dough scraper or spatula (it will be soft and sticky). Knead dough about 10 minutes, adding flour as needed to prevent sticking, until dough is smooth and very elastic. Place in large greased bowl; turn dough greased side up. Cover; let rise in cool place at least 3 hours or until tripled in size (or let rise 1 hour at room temperature and refrigerate overnight).

❷ Punch dough down. Cover; let rise 1½ to 2½ hours or until doubled in size. Turn dough out onto lightly floured surface. Divide into 3 equal pieces. To form each loaf, pat dough into an oval, then fold lengthwise into thirds. With side of hand, firmly press a trough down center of piece lengthwise; fold over and pinch seams together firmly. Roll each piece, starting from center and working outward until each loaf is 15 inches long.

❸ Grease 2 large baking sheets. Place 2 loaves on 1 sheet and the last loaf on the second sheet. Cover; let rise 45 minutes or until doubled in size. Heat oven to 450°F. Place 13x9-inch pan filled with boiling water on bottom rack or floor of oven. With sharp serrated knife or razor blade, slash each loaf diagonally 3 to 4 times across top; spritz with water or glaze with egg mixture. Bake 20 to 25 minutes or until crusty and browned. Cool on wire racks.

24 servings.
Preparation time: 6 hours, 25 minutes.
Ready to serve: 6 hours, 45 minutes.
Per serving: 115 calories, 0.5 g total fat (0 g saturated fat), 0 mg cholesterol, 290 mg sodium, 1 g fiber.

SHAPING YOUR BREAD

Enter a French boulangerie (bakery) and the shapes and sizes of breads can be mind-boggling. Here's a quick glossary of the most common ways that French bread dough can be formed:

•**Baguette.** French word for rod or wand. Long narrow loaf with diagonally slashed top.

•**Ficelle.** Shorter and skinnier than a baguette.

•**Boule.** Ball.

•**Bâtard.** Fat, log-shaped loaf with tapered ends, slashed top — often has nuts, raisins, or other stir-ins.

•**L'épis.** Shaft-of-wheat shape.

•**Couronne.** Crown shape.

•**Tordu.** Twisted baguette.

•**Torpedo.** Fat cigar-shaped loaf with tapered ends.

•**Petit Pain.** Small hard rolls.

MULTIGRAIN BREADS

Here's a collection of good-for-you breads that everyone will relish — no doorstop loaves in the bunch! These healthy breads are full of nature's goodness and abundance, from sweet potatoes, apples, nuts and raisins to a cereal basket of wholesome grains. Moist and dense, whole grain and hearty breads tend to be good keepers and make great toast down to the last heel.

Hoska, page 69

PPLE CINNAMON PECAN BREAD

It's not that common to see fresh apples in a yeast bread, but the sweet and tender chunks keep this whole wheat bread moist. Though bursting with apples and toasted pecans, the aroma of cinnamon is what will lure people into the kitchen to try these loaves.

1	(¼-oz.) pkg. active dry yeast	2	eggs
¼	cup honey	2½	teaspoons ground cinnamon
1½	cups warm apple cider or juice (105°F to 115°F)	2	teaspoons salt
3	cups whole wheat flour	1½ to 2	cups unbleached bread or all-purpose flour
2	cups pared chopped tart apples	½ to ¾	cup wheat bran
1	cup chopped toasted pecans		
2	tablespoons melted butter or vegetable oil		

❶ In large bowl, dissolve yeast and honey in apple cider; let stand 5 minutes. Add 2 cups of the whole wheat flour; beat until smooth. Cover; let stand 1 hour or until sponge is bubbly and risen.

❷ Add apples, pecans, butter, eggs, cinnamon, salt and remaining 1 cup whole wheat flour to sponge; beat until creamy. Stir in bread flour, ½ cup at a time, until soft dough forms that just clears sides of bowl. Turn dough out onto lightly floured surface. Knead 5 minutes or until smooth and elastic. Push back any apples or nuts that fall out during kneading. Place in greased bowl; turn dough greased side up. Cover; let rise in warm place 1½ to 2 hours or until doubled in size.

❸ Grease 2 (9x5-inch) loaf pans. Punch down dough. Sprinkle work surface with bran. Turn dough out onto surface, rolling it in bran. Divide dough into 4 equal pieces. Roll each piece into 12-inch rope. Twist 2 ropes together; pinch ends together and place in 1 loaf pan. Repeat with remaining 2 ropes. Cover; let rise 45 minutes or until doubled in size. Heat oven to 350°F. Bake 45 to 50 minutes or until golden brown. Remove from pans; cool on wire rack.

24 servings.

Preparation time: 35 minutes.

Ready to serve: 3 hours, 45 minutes.

Per serving: 155 calories, 5 g total fat (1 g saturated fat), 20 mg cholesterol, 205 mg sodium, 3.5 g fiber.

BAKER'S NOTES

• An electric standing mixer works well with this dough. Beginning with a sponge, a mixer makes short work of beating in the chopped apples, nuts and flour.

• Tart cooking apples hold their shape and flavor during baking, yet become very tender. Granny Smith, Newton Pippin, Golden Delicious, Rome Beauty, Jonagold, Cortland, Jonathon and Macintosh are among the best.

WESTPHALIAN PUMPERNICKEL BREAD

Sometimes called Russian black bread, dark pumpernickel is said to have its true roots in 15th century Germany. Thinly sliced and served with cheese, dark pumpernickel makes a nice appetizer.

2 (¼-oz.) pkg. active dry yeast
2½ cups warm water (105°F to 115°F)
⅓ cup butter, softened
¼ cup dark molasses
¼ cup distilled or apple cider vinegar
3 tablespoons unsweetened cocoa
1 tablespoon fennel seeds
1 tablespoon instant coffee granules
2 teaspoons salt

4 cups dark rye flour
1 cup hominy grits or cornmeal, plus additional for dusting baking sheet
3 cups unbleached bread flour
1 cup raisins or snipped pitted dried plums (prunes)
1 teaspoon cornstarch
½ cup water

❶ In large bowl, dissolve yeast in ½ cup of the water; let stand 5 minutes. Stir in remaining 2 cups water, butter, molasses, vinegar, cocoa, fennel seeds, coffee granules and salt; mix well.

❷ Gradually stir in rye flour, 1 cup hominy and 1 cup of the bread flour; mix well to form soft dough. Turn dough out onto surface dusted with 1 cup bread flour. Knead 5 minutes; cover and let rest 15 minutes. Knead in remaining 1 cup bread flour 10 to 15 minutes longer or until smooth and elastic. Place in greased bowl; turn dough greased side up. Cover; let rise in warm place 1 to 1½ hours or until doubled in size.

❸ Sprinkle hominy on baking sheet(s). Punch dough down; turn out onto lightly floured surface. Knead in raisins. Divide dough in half. Shape each half into 5-inch balls; place on baking sheet(s) or in greased 8-inch round pans. Cover; let rise 1 hour or until doubled in size.

❹ Heat oven to 350°F. Slash large cross on top of each loaf with sharp serrated knife or razor blade. Bake 50 minutes or until bread sounds hollow when tapped. Meanwhile, mix cornstarch and ½ cup water in small saucepan. Cook over medium heat, stirring constantly, 1 minute. As soon as bread is baked, brush cornstarch mixture over top of loaves. Return to oven; bake an additional 2 to 3 minutes longer or until glaze is set. Cool on wire rack.

32 servings.
Preparation time: 1 hour, 5 minutes.
Ready to serve: 3 hours, 30 minutes.
Per serving: 155 calories, 2.5 g total fat (1.5 g saturated fat), 5 mg cholesterol, 160 mg sodium, 3 g fiber.

MULTIGRAIN PEASANT BREAD

This healthful loaf has a nutty flavor and crunchy texture as a result of the addition of cracked multi-grain cereal and rolled oat granola.

½ cup boiling water

⅓ cup seven-grain cereal, plus
　　additional for sprinkling loaf

2 tablespoons each vegetable oil, honey

1 teaspoon salt

1 (¼-oz.) pkg. active dry yeast

½ cup warm water (105°F to 115°F)

1 cup granola cereal, crushed

1 egg

2½ to 3 cups whole wheat flour

1 egg white beaten with 1
　　tablespoon water

Cornmeal

❶ In large bowl, mix boiling water and ⅓ cup seven-grain cereal; let stand until cooled. Add oil, honey and salt.

❷ In small bowl, dissolve yeast in water; let stand 5 minutes. Stir into cereal mixture with granola, egg and enough of the whole wheat flour to make stiff dough; let rest 15 minutes. Turn dough out onto lightly floured surface. Knead 5 minutes or until smooth. Place in greased bowl; turn dough greased side up. Cover; let rise in warm place 1½ hours or until doubled in size.

❸ Dust large baking sheet with cornmeal. Punch dough down; turn out onto lightly floured surface. Shape into tight round loaf (about 5 inches); place on baking sheet. Cover; let rise 1 hour or until doubled. Heat oven to 400°F, with baking stone on bottom oven rack, if desired. With sharp serrated knife or razor blade, slash an "X" on top of dough. Brush with egg white mixture; sprinkle with seven-grain cereal. Slide loaf onto baking stone or keep on baking sheet. Bake 25 minutes or until dark golden brown. Cool on wire rack.

16 servings.

Preparation time: 30 minutes.

Ready to serve: 3 hours, 15 minutes.

Per serving: 140 calories, 4 g total fat (1.5 g saturated fat), 15 mg cholesterol, 155 mg sodium, 3.5 g fiber.

GERMAN TRIPLE ONION CRESCENT

This moist whole grain loaf has a deep onion flavor and aroma. Split in half horizontally and fill with sliced sausage, strong cheeses and hot German mustard or horseradish — then slice the horseshoe-shaped loaf into individual servings for entertaining.

1	(¼-oz.) pkg. active dry yeast	¾	cup thinly sliced leek
2	cups whole wheat flour	1½ to 2	cups unbleached bread flour
2	tablespoons packed brown sugar	1¼	teaspoons salt
1¼	cups dark beer		Cornmeal
3	tablespoons vegetable oil	1	egg beaten with 1 tablespoon water
1	tablespoon butter		
¾	cup thinly sliced yellow onion		Mustard seeds
¾	cup thinly sliced red onion		

❶ Place yeast, 1 cup of the whole wheat flour, brown sugar, beer and 2 tablespoons of the oil in 1½-lb. loaf bread machine, following manufacturer's instructions. Select Dough cycle; press Start.

❷ Meanwhile, in large skillet, heat remaining 1 tablespoon oil and butter over medium heat. Sauté yellow onion, red onion and leek 15 minutes or until golden brown. Cool.

❸ When dough cycle is complete, add remaining 1 cup whole wheat flour, 1½ cups of the bread flour, salt and onion mixture to bread machine pan. Process on Dough cycle once more (dough will rise to top of pan). Sprinkle large baking sheet with cornmeal. Turn dough out onto floured surface; knead dough 2 minutes, adding enough remaining ½ cup bread flour to prevent sticking as needed. Shape dough into 18- to 20-inch log; lay on baking sheet and curve into horseshoe-shape. Cover; let rise 30 minutes or until nearly doubled in size. Heat oven to 400°F. Brush dough with egg mixture; sprinkle with mustard seeds. Bake 20 to 25 minutes or until deep golden brown. Cool on wire rack.

16 servings.
Preparation time: 40 minutes.
Ready to serve: 4 hours, 30 minutes.
Per serving: 150 calories, 4 g total fat (1 g saturated fat), 10 mg cholesterol, 195 mg sodium, 2.5 g fiber.

BAKER'S NOTES
- If preferred, use all yellow or red onions. The key to the best flavor in this bread is slowly cooking onions to caramelize their natural sugars.
- Be sure to thoroughly wash out any sand lurking in the leek layers. Slice the bottom white part of the leek, rather than the tough upper green leaves.

FRAGRANT ANADAMA BREAD

A sturdy American classic, this cornmeal loaf dates back to colonial New England.

1 cup water	⅓ cup whole grain millet
½ cup stone-ground (coarse) yellow cornmeal	1½ teaspoons salt
1 (¼-oz.) pkg. active dry yeast	4½ to 5 cups unbleached bread flour
1 cup warm water (105°F to 115°F)	Cornmeal
¼ cup each, softened butter, sorghum or molasses	

❶ Put 1 cup water in small saucepan over medium heat. Slowly pour in ½ cup cornmeal mixture and cook, stirring constantly, 2 minutes or until thick. Cool. In large bowl, dissolve yeast in water; let stand 5 minutes. Stir in cornmeal, butter, sorghum, millet and salt. Stir in bread flour, 1 cup at a time, beating vigorously until dough is very stiff and sticky (about 3½ cups).

❷ Turn dough out onto surface dusted with 1 cup bread flour. Using dough scraper or spatula, fold dough over and coat with flour. Knead 8 minutes or until smooth and elastic, using only enough flour to prevent sticking. Place in greased bowl; turn dough greased side up. Cover; let rise in warm place 1 to 1½ hours or until doubled in size.

❸ Grease 2 (8x4-inch) loaf pans; dust insides with cornmeal. Punch dough down; divide in half. Shape each half into 1 loaf; place in pans. With sharp serrated knife or razor blade, make 3 diagonal slashes on top of each loaf. Cover; let rise 45 minutes or until doubled in size. Heat oven to 350°F. Bake 35 minutes or until deep golden brown and loaves sound hollow when tapped. Remove from pans; cool on wire rack.

24 servings.
Preparation time: 30 minutes.
Ready to serve: 3 hours, 15 minutes.
Per serving: 145 calories, 2.5 g total fat (1.5 g saturated fat), 5 mg cholesterol, 160 mg sodium, 1 g fiber.

BAKER'S NOTE

• Many recipes call for slashing dough just before baking. By slashing these loaves before the last rise, the dough opens up more and creates a dramatic appearance after baking.

SUNFLOWER MAPLE WHEAT TWIST

I love the yin and yang appearance of this bread — a white dough twisted with a whole wheat dough, so that each slice offers a bit of both.

DOUGH

¾ cup water

⅓ cup bulgur (cracked wheat)

2 (¼-oz.) pkg. active dry yeast

¼ cup warm water (105°F to 115°F)

2 tablespoons butter, softened

⅓ cup maple syrup

2 teaspoons salt

1 egg

2¾ to 3 cups unbleached all-purpose flour

¾ to 1 cup whole wheat flour

½ cup unsalted sunflower seeds

MAPLE-SUNFLOWER GLAZE

¼ cup unsalted sunflower seeds

1 tablespoon butter

¼ cup maple syrup

2 tablespoons sugar

❶ In small saucepan, heat ¾ cup water just to boiling. Stir in bulgur; cool. In large bowl, dissolve yeast in water; let stand 5 minutes. Stir in softened butter, ⅓ cup maple syrup, salt, egg, bulgur mixture and 2 cups of the all-purpose flour. Beat until smooth.

❷ Divide dough in half. Stir in enough of the whole wheat flour to 1 dough half to form soft dough. Stir in enough remaining all-purpose flour to other half to form soft dough. Turn each dough half out onto lightly floured surface; knead each 5 minutes. Flatten each half; sprinkle each with ¼ cup sunflower seeds. Fold dough halves over and gently knead seeds in until well distributed. Place dough in greased bowls; turn greased sides up. Cover; let rise in warm place 1 to 1½ hours or until doubled in size.

❸ Grease large baking sheet. Punch doughs down; turn out onto lightly floured surface. Roll each half into 15-inch rope. Place ropes side by side on baking sheet. Twist together gently and loosely. Press ends to seal. Cover; let rise 1 hour or until doubled in size. Heat oven to 350°F. Bake 30 to 35 minutes or until golden brown.

❹ Meanwhile, prepare glaze: In medium skillet over medium-high heat, cook and stir sunflower seeds in 1 tablespoon butter until golden brown. Stir in ¼ cup maple syrup and sugar; heat to boiling, stirring constantly. Remove from heat; cool.

❺ Remove bread from oven; cool 5 minutes. Spread with glaze.

16 servings.

Preparation time: 35 minutes.

Ready to serve: 1 hour, 30 minutes.

Per serving: 205 calories, 6 g total fat (2 g saturated fat), 20 mg cholesterol, 310 mg sodium, 3 g fiber.

SPICED SWEET POTATO BREAD

Like in other potato breads, mashed sweet potato add moistness and staying power to whole grain breads, which can dry out quickly. Serve thick slices with cream cheese and marmalade or spiced apple butter.

2	cups milk	¼	cup packed dark brown sugar
¼	cup butter	1½	cups mashed cooked sweet potato
1	(¼-oz.) pkg. active dry yeast	2	teaspoons grated lemon peel
¼	cup warm water (105°F to 115°F)	1½	teaspoons salt
3½ to 4	cups unbleached all-purpose flour	1¼	teaspoons pumpkin pie spice
3½	cups whole wheat flour		Softened butter

❶ In medium saucepan, heat milk and butter just until warm (105°F to 115°F).

❷ In large bowl, dissolve yeast in water; let stand 5 minutes. Stir in milk mixture, 2 cups of the all-purpose flour, whole wheat flour, sugar, sweet potato, lemon peel, salt and pumpkin pie spice. Beat at medium speed, scraping bowl often, 1 to 2 minutes or until smooth. By hand, stir in enough remaining flour to create manageable dough. Turn dough out onto lightly floured surface. Knead 6 to 8 minutes or until smooth and elastic. Place in greased bowl; turn dough greased side up. Cover; let rise in warm place 1 hour or until doubled in size.

❸ Grease baking sheets. Punch dough down. Turn out onto lightly floured surface; divide in half. Shape each half into tight round loaf (about 6 inches). Place loaves on baking sheets; cover and let rise 1 hour or until doubled in size. Heat oven to 350°F. Bake 35 to 45 minutes or until loaves sound hollow when tapped. Cool on wire racks. Brush tops of loaves with softened butter.

24 servings.

Preparation time: 25 minutes.

Ready to serve: 2 hours, 30 minutes.

Per serving: 180 calories, 3 g total fat (1.5 g saturated fat), 10 mg cholesterol, 175 mg sodium, 3 g fiber.

BAKER'S NOTES

• One-half teaspoon ground cinnamon, ½ teaspoon ground ginger, ¼ teaspoon ground cloves and a dash of ground nutmeg can be substituted for the pumpkin pie spice.

• Look for Ruby or Jewell yams (which are actually sweet potatoes). Both have bright orange flesh and are very moist and sweet. Boil or bake to mash for this bread. Or substitute canned, cooked sweet potatoes packed in water, not syrup.

• Other starchy winter squash varieties can be substituted for the sweet potato — try cooked butternut squash or fresh pumpkin.

OATMEAL MOLASSES HEARTH BREAD

Batter breads give you homemade goodness without having to knead dough. Plus, there is only a single rising. The texture is coarser than kneaded bread, but this loaf is delicious and makes great toast too.

½ cup milk	1 egg
⅓ cup water	2½ cups whole wheat flour
⅓ cup molasses	1 cup old-fashioned rolled oats, toasted
3 tablespoons vegetable oil	
1½ teaspoons salt	2 tablespoons honey
1 (¼-oz.) pkg. active dry yeast	

❶ Grease 9x5-inch loaf pan. In medium saucepan or in microwave, heat milk, water, molasses, oil and salt to lukewarm. Pour into large bowl. Dissolve yeast in warm mixture; let stand 5 minutes.

❷ With electric mixer, beat in egg. Gradually beat in flour and ¾ cup of the oats, mixing 4 minutes or until smooth and elastic. Scrape batter into pan, smoothing top with wet fingers. Cover; let rise in warm place 1½ to 2 hours or until dough nearly reaches top of pan.

❸ Heat oven to 350°F. Bake 40 to 45 minutes or until loaf is crusty and deep golden brown (if loaf begins browning too quickly, tent with foil during last 15 minutes of baking). Brush warm loaf with honey; sprinkle with remaining ¼ cup toasted oats. Cool 5 minutes; remove from pan. Cool on wire rack.

16 servings.
Preparation time: 20 minutes.
Ready to serve: 2 hours, 25 minutes.

Per serving: 140 calories, 3.5 g total fat (0.5 g saturated fat), 15 mg cholesterol, 230 mg sodium, 3 g fiber.

BAKER'S NOTE

• Toast rolled oats in an ungreased 13x9-inch pan in a 350°F oven 6 to 8 minutes or until light brown, stirring once.

ℋOSKA

This bread (pronounced hoe-ska) is adapted from a family recipe given to me by my editor's mother, Doris Carpenter. It's an old country-style loaf that is Eastern European (Bohemia, to be specific) in origin, and shows off the virtuosity of the accomplished country baker.

2	(¼-oz.) pkg. active dry yeast	1	cup golden raisins
2	cups warm water (105°F to 115°F)	1	cup chopped pecans or black walnuts
½	cup peanut or vegetable oil	1/2	cup currants
½	cup sugar	2	egg yolks beaten with 1/4 cup water
1½	teaspoons salt		
2	eggs, slightly beaten	¾ to 1	cup toasted wheat germ
7¾ to 8¼	cups unbleached bread flour		

❶ In large bowl, dissolve yeast in water; let stand 10 minutes. Stir in oil, sugar, salt, eggs and 3 cups of the flour; beat until smooth. Let sponge stand 30 minutes or until bubbly and risen.

❷ Stir raisins, pecans and currants into sponge. Stir in remaining flour, 1 cup at a time, beating well until soft dough forms (about 4 cups). Turn dough out onto floured surface. Knead 20 minutes; work in flour as needed to form smooth and elastic dough. Push back any dried fruit or nuts that fall out of dough. Place in greased bowl; turn dough greased side up. Cover; let rise in warm place 1 hour or until doubled in size. Punch down dough; re-cover and let rise 1 hour longer.

❸ Grease 2 large baking sheets. Turn dough out onto lightly floured surface. Divide dough in half; cover 1 half with bowl and let rest while braiding first loaf. For first half, divide into 2 unequal parts, ⅔ to ⅓ dough. Divide larger piece into 3 pieces; roll into 15-inch ropes. Divide smaller piece into 3 pieces; roll into 10-inch ropes. Brush ropes with egg yolk mixture; sprinkle with wheat germ.

❹ Braid each set of 3 ropes, so you have 2 braids. Place larger braid on baking sheet. Lay smaller braid on top; press gently to seal onto larger braid. Cover; let rise in warm place 30 to 45 minutes or until nearly doubled in size. Repeat with remaining half of dough. Sprinkle braids with any remaining wheat germ. Heat oven to 350°F. Bake 40 to 45 minutes or until golden brown (tent with foil during last 15 minutes to minutes to prevent excessive browning).

32 servings.
Preparation time: 1 hour, 15 minutes.
Ready to serve: 5 hours, 30 minutes.
Per serving: 230 calories, 7 g total fat (1 g saturated fat), 25 mg cholesterol, 115 mg sodium, 2 g fiber.

ORANGE 'N SPICE RYE BREAD

Rye bread, flavored with orange and caraway, is a favorite during the Christmas holidays in Sweden. This light rye is nice year 'round, with a flavor twist that includes cumin and anise seeds.

1 (¼-oz.) pkg. active dry yeast	½ teaspoon toasted anise seeds
¼ cup warm water (105°F to 115°F)	¾ teaspoon salt
¾ cup lukewarm orange juice	1 cup medium rye flour
1 egg	2½ to 3 cups unbleached bread flour
3 tablespoons light molasses	1 egg white beaten with 1 tablespoon water
1 tablespoon butter, softened	
1 teaspoon grated orange peel	Cumin seeds and/or anise seeds, if desired
1 teaspoon toasted cumin seeds	

❶ In large bowl, dissolve yeast in water; let stand 5 minutes. Add orange juice, egg, molasses, butter, orange peel, 1 teaspoon cumin seeds, ½ teaspoon anise seeds, salt, rye flour and 1 cup of the bread flour. Beat at low speed 30 seconds; beat at high speed 3 minutes. By hand, stir in as much remaining bread flour as needed to create soft dough.

❷ Turn dough out onto lightly floured surface. Knead 8 minutes, adding bread flour as needed to make moderately stiff dough that is smooth and elastic. Place in greased bowl; turn dough greased side up. Cover; let rise in warm place 1 hour or until doubled in size.

❸ Line large baking sheet with parchment paper. Punch dough down. Shape into oblong loaf, tapering ends. Place on baking sheet. Cover; let rise 30 to 45 minutes or until nearly doubled in size. Heat oven to 375°F. With sharp serrated knife or razor blade, slash top of dough as desired; brush with egg white mixture. Sprinkle with seeds. Bake 30 minutes or until lightly browned. Cool on wire rack.

16 servings.
Preparation time: 45 minutes.
Ready to serve: 2 hours.
Per serving: 130 calories, 1.5 g total fat (0.5 g saturated fat), 15 mg cholesterol, 125 mg sodium, 1.5 g fiber.

BAKER'S NOTES

• Because this dough makes a single loaf, it would be a good option for being made in the bread machine. Place ingredients in 1½-lb. loaf bread machine, following manufacturer's instructions. Select Dough cycle; press Start. When it's ready, shape and bake dough as directed (Step 3).

• To toast cumin and anise seeds, place seeds in dry skillet. Cook over medium heat 1 to 2 minutes or until seeds are aromatic and color just begins to darken.

MOIST BARLEY BREAD

The cooked barley gives a totally different texture than using just barley flour. This bread is extremely satisfying with a cup of thick, hot soup.

2	(¼-oz.) pkg. active dry yeast	¼	teaspoon dried thyme
2	tablespoons honey	¼	teaspoon baking soda
½	cup warm water (105°F to 115°F)	3	cups unbleached all-purpose flour
2	cups lukewarm buttermilk	2¼	cups whole wheat flour
1	tablespoon light olive or vegetable oil	1	cup cooked pearled barley or wheat berries
1	teaspoon salt		Cornmeal
½	teaspoon dried rosemary	1	egg beaten with 1 tablespoon milk

❶ In large bowl, dissolve yeast and honey in water; let stand 5 minutes. Add buttermilk, oil, salt, rosemary, thyme, baking soda and all-purpose flour; beat at low speed until moistened. With electric mixer, beat 3 minutes at medium speed, scraping bowl occasionally. By hand, stir in whole wheat flour and barley until stiff batter forms.

❷ Grease 2 (8x4-inch) loaf pans; sprinkle with cornmeal. Divide batter evenly between pans. Smooth tops of loaves by patting with floured hands. Cover; let rise in warm place 30 minutes or until batter is at top of pans. Heat oven to 400°F. Brush dough with egg mixture; sprinkle with cornmeal. Bake 30 to 35 minutes or until golden brown. Remove from pans; cool on wire rack.

24 servings.
Preparation time: 30 minutes.
Ready to serve: 2 hours.
Per serving: 130 calories, 1.5 g total fat (0.5 g saturated fat), 10 mg cholesterol, 130 mg sodium, 2.5 g fiber.

VARIATION Kasha Bread
Substitute cooked kasha (buckwheat groats) for barley. Cook as directed on package.

BAKER'S NOTE
• To cook pearled barley or wheat berries, simmer grains in twice the amount of water one hour or until tender. Quick-cooking barley is also available; it takes only 10 minutes to cook.

ILD RICE L'EPIS

L'épis (pronounced lay-pee) are the long, branchy loaves of French bread that resemble shafts of wheat. Wild rice, which is actually a wild grass, grows on similar long stalks. The kernels of wild rice are stripped off either by hand or mechanically.

1	(¼-oz.) pkg. active dry yeast	2	cups whole wheat flour
½	cup warm water (105°F to 115°F)	1	cup old-fashioned rolled oats
2	cups chicken broth	4¼ to 4½	cups unbleached bread flour
2	tablespoons olive oil	2	cups cooked wild rice
1½	teaspoons salt		Cornmeal
¾	teaspoon dried thyme	1	egg beaten with 1 tablespoon water
3	garlic cloves, minced		

❶ In large bowl, dissolve yeast in water; let stand 5 minutes. Add broth, oil, salt, thyme and garlic. Stir in whole wheat flour, oats and 2 cups of the bread flour; mix until soft dough forms. Stir in wild rice. Cover dough; let rest 15 minutes. Stir in enough remaining bread flour to create stiff dough. Turn dough out onto lightly floured surface. Knead 10 minutes or until smooth and elastic. Place in greased bowl; turn dough greased side up. Cover; let rise in warm place 1½ hours or until doubled in size.

❷ Sprinkle 2 large baking sheets with cornmeal. Punch dough down. Turn out onto lightly floured surface. Divide dough into fourths. Roll each piece into 12x8-inch rectangle; roll up to form 12-inch-long baguettes. Place on baking sheets. Snip dough with kitchen shears at 45-degree angle, halfway through baguettes at 3-inch intervals. Alternate twisting pieces from side to side to resemble shaft of wheat. Cover; let rise 30 minutes or until puffy.

❸ Heat oven to 400°F. Brush loaves with egg mixture; bake 25 to 30 minutes or until golden brown. Spray inside of oven with water several times during first 10 minutes of baking for crustier loaves. Cool on wire racks.

32 servings.
Preparation time: 45 minutes.
Ready to serve: 3 hours.

Per serving: 125 calories, 1.5 g total fat (0.5 g saturated fat), 5 mg cholesterol, 180 mg sodium, 2 g fiber.

BAKER'S NOTES

- Cook about 1 cup uncooked wild rice, covered, in 2 cups water about 55 minutes to yield 2 cups cooked rice. For this bread, be sure to cook rice until kernels burst and are very tender. Canned or frozen cooked wild rice could be substituted.

- Brown rice or wehani, a cultivated brown rice hybrid that is red in color, could be substituted for wild rice. Look for wehani rice at natural food stores or co-op groceries.

- Don't overproof snipped baguettes before baking. If they get too "risen," the branched look of the loaves will be lost.

SOURDOUGH BREADS

From the beginning of bread-making history, the story of sourdough breads has fascinated dedicated bakers. Using sourdough starters can add a new dimension, and a bit of a challenge, to your baking. Experiment with the following recipes and learn to vary your starter pot, lending more or less of a sour flavor to your breads, pancakes and biscuits.

Sun-Dried Tomato Bâtards, page 87

INER'S SOURDOUGH STARTER

I grew up in a Western family that treasures its sourdough starter. Here are some recipes for starting your own family tradition. Depending on who you talk to, you hear many opinions of the best way to begin a starter — water-based or milk-based, using a bit of commercial yeast or not …

WATER-BASED STARTER

½   teaspoon active dry yeast, if desired (this just speeds up the fermentation process)

2   tablespoons sugar

2   cups thick potato water*

About 2 cups unbleached bread flour

❶ In large bowl, dissolve yeast and sugar in warm potato water. Beat in flour until smooth. Pour batter into large glass jar, plastic container or ceramic crock. Cover with plastic wrap and clean kitchen towel or double layer of cheesecloth.

❷ Let batter stand in warm place (at room temperature, ideally 80°F) at least 3 days, stirring occasionally, until starter has a nice sour smell and looks active (tiny bubbles on surface of batter). Starter can be used in recipes at this point. Or stir in 1 tablespoon sugar, 2 tablespoons flour and more water if batter seems too thick; let stand another 3 or 4 days or until really bubbly. The longer the starter ferments, the better the flavor of your baked goods. Refrigerate starter pot until ready to use.

3 cups.

TIP *To make potato water: Simmer 1 medium-sized russet potato in 2 to 3 cups water until it falls apart. Remove potato skin, mash potato well and add 1½ cups of the cooking liquid to make a thick potato "water." (The proportion is about 1 cup mashed potato to 1½ cups water.)

MILK-BASED STARTER

1½   cups lukewarm (about 80°F) nonfat milk

¼   teaspoon active dry yeast

1   teaspoon sugar

2   cups unbleached bread flour

¼   cup water

❶ In large bowl, combine milk, yeast, sugar and 1½ cups of the flour; stir until smooth. Cover with plastic wrap; let stand at room temperature (about 80°F) at least 72 hours (3 days).

❷ After 3 days, stir in water and remaining ½ cup flour; cover and let stand 2 hours or until very bubbly, with a sour aroma. Use starter as desired in recipes. Replenish (or feed) starter by stirring in ½ cup water and ½ cup flour; let stand several hours. Refrigerate until next use.

2 cups.

EUROPEAN SOURDOUGH STARTER

This starter is based on a style of sourdough common in Europe, very much like Italian biga. It tends to be more dough-like, rather than the looser batters found in the western United States. If you use only part of this starter, or don't plan to bake within four or five days of making it, discard any remaining starter and begin fresh when you are ready to bake again.

¼ teaspoon active dry yeast
1 cup warm water (105°F to 115°F)
2¼ cups unbleached bread flour

❶ In large bowl, dissolve yeast in water; let stand 5 minutes. Gradually stir in flour, beating until smooth and sticky soft dough forms. Cover with plastic wrap and towel. Let stand in warm place at least 4 hours or up to 24 hours. If not using immediately, loosely cover and refrigerate up to 3 days. Use as desired in recipes.

2 cups.

STARTER SECRETS

Here is some wisdom on working with sourdough starters.

- Authentic "sour dough" or pre-ferments is nothing more than a batter of flour and water or milk. Left to stand at room temperature, this batter captures the wild yeasts that feed off the flour; the gases they emit during their activity is what gives rise to baked goods. The sour or tangy flavor comes from good bacteria breaking down the sugars in flour and milk, producing acids. Fermentation also produces some carbon dioxide bubbles.

- Use hard wheat bread flour (preferably unbleached and organic) to make starters. The high gluten content of hard wheat, along with the sour starter, gives the characteristic dense, chewy texture associated with sourdough bread. The proportion of liquid to flour in a recipe also affects its texture.

- Give yourself time to work with sourdough — it takes time to develop the sour flavor, and the yeast works more slowly than commercial yeast, so longer rising times are necessary. To boost rising power, commercial active dry yeast can be added to breads, especially those using low-gluten flours (rye, barley, etc.).

- When making the starter, if a pink mold begins to grow on the batter, discard and begin again.

- Do not keep sourdough starter in a metal bowl — metal inhibits yeast activity.

- Keep the sourdough crock loosely covered in the refrigerator (covering with plastic wrap and sealing with a rubber band works well). The live yeasts in the starter emit gas as they do their work, and a tightly sealed container doesn't allow the gases to escape.

- Each time you use your starter, you must replenish it with equal amounts flour and water or milk. (If a recipe calls for 1 cup starter, then replenish pot with 1 cup flour and 1 cup liquid). Allow to stand at room temperature for several hours until bubbly, then re-store in refrigerator. If you don't use it at least once a week, you must "feed" it with flour and liquid at least once a month (double its volume, then give away some of it). If you won't use it for several weeks or more, it's better to freeze it. Leave starter at room temperature 24 hours after thawing, to awaken the dormant yeast.

SOURDOUGH ENGLISH MUFFINS

English muffins, distant American relations to the English crumpet, are firm griddle cakes that are best split and toasted. Made with sourdough, the toasted aroma is tangy, and the split rounds make a great base for favorites such as eggs benedict or melted cheese sandwiches.

½ cup *Miner's Sourdough Starter* (page 76)	1 tablespoon sugar
1 cup milk	¾ teaspoon salt
2¼ cups unbleached all-purpose flour	½ teaspoon baking soda
½ cup whole wheat flour	White or yellow cornmeal

❶ In large bowl, combine starter, milk and 2 cups of the all-purpose flour; mix well. Cover loosely; let stand at room temperature about 8 hours or overnight.

❷ Stir whole wheat flour, sugar, salt and baking soda into batter; beat until stiff dough forms. Turn dough out onto surface floured with remaining ¼ cup all-purpose flour. Knead several minutes or until no longer sticky, adding more all-purpose flour if needed.

❸ Roll dough to ¾-inch thickness. Cut out 12 rounds with 3-inch cutter. Place on cornmeal-dusted baking sheet. Cover; let rise 45 minutes or until puffy.

❹ Heat griddle or large nonstick skillet over medium heat. Bake muffins 8 to 10 minutes per side, turning once. Serve warm from griddle, or split and toast.

13 servings.
Preparation time: 35 minutes.
Ready to serve: 10 hours, 5 minutes.
Per serving: 125 calories, 0.5 g fat (0.5 g saturated fat), 0 mg cholesterol, 195 mg sodium, 1.5 g fiber.

VARIATION   Cinnamon Raisin English Muffins

Substitute 3 tablespoons packed brown sugar for the 1 tablespoon sugar, and stir ½ up raisins and 1 teaspoon ground cinnamon into dough in Step 2.

KLONDIKE BISCUITS

Western miners would live on these biscuits, day in and out, when food was scarce. If bacon was available, or a bit of tough beef steak that could be parlayed into gravy after cooking, the miner would consider himself lucky. During the gold rush days of the 1800's, a woman could make a tidy sum of money baking fresh biscuits for hungry miners — sometimes an easier way to strike it rich!

2   cups unbleached all-purpose flour
1   teaspoon baking powder
½   teaspoon each baking soda
½   teaspoon salt
⅓   cup lard or butter
½   cup *Miner's Sourdough Starter*
     (page 76)
     About ½ cup buttermilk or sour
     milk

❶ Heat oven to 425°F. In large bowl, mix flour, baking powder, baking soda and salt. Cut lard into mixture with pastry blender until mixture resembles small crumbs.

❷ Stir in starter and enough buttermilk to make soft dough. Turn dough out onto floured surface. Knead lightly about 1 minute. Roll or pat dough out to ½-inch thickness. Cut with round cutters or rim of glass (about 2½ to 3 inches). Place on baking sheet. Bake 10 to 12 minutes or until lightly browned.

12 servings.
Preparation time: 35 minutes.
Ready to serve: 1 hour.
Per serving: 150 calories, 6 g fat (2.5 g saturated fat), 5 mg cholesterol, 200 mg sodium, 0.5 g fiber.

DILLED SOUR RYE BREAD

This unique bread takes advantage of dilled pickle brine — vinegar adds more sourness to the bread crumb, and dillweed enhances the overall dill flavor — making this an intensely flavored loaf. Using additional yeast speeds up the rise time — though for a more sour flavor, you can let the sponge stand overnight.

1 cup *Miner's Sourdough Starter* (page 76)	1 egg
½ cup warm dill pickle brine (about 90°F)	1 tablespoon dry dillweed
1½ cups rye flour	2 teaspoons caraway seeds
1 (¼-oz.) pkg. active dry yeast	1 teaspoon salt
¼ cup warm water (105°F to 115°F)	2¼ to 2½ cups unbleached bread flour
2 tablespoons vegetable oil	Cornmeal
	1 egg beaten with 1 teaspoon water

❶ In large bowl, mix starter with pickle brine and 1 cup of the rye flour. For sourest flavor, cover and let stand in warm place 12 hours or up to 24 hours. If time is short, continue making dough.

❷ In small bowl, dissolve yeast in water; let stand 5 minutes. Stir into starter mixture with remaining ½ cup rye flour, oil, egg, dillweed, caraway and salt; beat until smooth.

❸ Stir in enough bread flour to create manageable dough. Turn dough out onto floured surface. Knead 8 to 10 minutes or until smooth and elastic. Place dough in greased bowl; turn greased side up. Cover; let rise in warm place 2 hours or until doubled in size.

❹ Punch dough down; divide in half. Form each half into 15-inch rope. Place on cornmeal-dusted baking sheet. Twist ropes together; turn ends under to seal. Cover; let rise 40 minutes or until puffy. Heat oven to 375°F. Brush dough with egg mixture. Bake 30 to 35 minutes or until golden brown. Cool on wire rack.

16 servings.

Preparation time: 40 minutes.

Ready to serve: 4 hours, 20 minutes.

Per serving: 155 calories, 2.5 g fat (0.5 g saturated fat), 25 mg cholesterol, 185 mg sodium, 2.5 g fiber.

BAKER'S NOTES
- Warm pickle brine gently on the stovetop or in the microwave.
- Dried minced onion could be sprinkled over top of the loaf before baking.

TUSCAN ROASTED GRAPE FLATBREAD

A rustic, layered flatbread is traditionally made during the Sangiovese grape harvest in Tuscany. Fresh red grapes dot the top of this light dough, while raisins macerated in Vin Santo (a local fortified wine made from the lees of the grape crush) are sandwiched in between. Here, the raisins are marinated in an orange-flavored fortified wine.

1 cup dark or golden raisins	½ cup packed brown sugar
½ cup orange Muscat or late harvest Riesling wine	3 tablespoons olive oil
2 teaspoons active dry yeast	1 teaspoon salt
¾ cup warm water (105°F to 115°F)	Cornmeal
1 cup *European Sourdough Starter* (page 77)	2 cups small red seedless grapes
2¾ cups unbleached bread flour	1 teaspoon fennel seeds

❶ In small bowl, combine raisins and orange Muscat; let stand several hours. Drain well and reserve. In large bowl, dissolve yeast in water; let stand 5 minutes. Stir in starter, flour, ⅓ cup of the brown sugar, oil and salt; beat until soft, sticky dough forms. Turn dough out onto lightly floured surface. Knead 8 to 10 minutes or until smooth and elastic. Place dough in greased bowl; turn greased side up. Cover; let rise in warm place 1½ to 2 hours or until doubled in size.

❷ Dust large baking sheet with cornmeal. Punch dough down. Turn out onto lightly floured surface; knead briefly. Let rest 10 minutes. Divide dough in half. Roll each half into 9½-inch round. Place 1 round on baking sheet. Spread drained raisins evenly over round of dough on baking sheet. Place second dough round on top, pinching edges to seal. Cover; let rise 30 minutes or until doubled in size.

❸ Heat oven to 400°F. Cover dough evenly with grapes, lightly pressing them into dough. Sprinkle with remaining brown sugar (about 3 tablespoons) and fennel seeds. Bake 40 to 45 minutes or until bread is golden brown and grapes are lightly browned. Cool on wire rack; serve warm.

16 servings.

Preparation time: 40 minutes.

Ready to serve: 3 hours, 50 minutes.

Per serving: 220 calories, 3 g fat (0.5 g saturated fat), 0 mg cholesterol, 150 mg sodium, 1.5 g fiber.

USTIC SOURDOUGH HEALTH BREAD

The list of ingredients for this dense, grainy loaf may seem daunting, but all are readily available in the baking section of the grocery store.

1 cup *European Sourdough Starter* (page 77)	2 tablespoons olive oil
1½ cups warm milk (105°F to 115°F)	½ cup old-fashioned rolled oats
3¼ to 3½ cups unbleached bread flour	½ cup bulgur (cracked wheat)
1 (¼-oz.) pkg. active dry yeast	½ cup stone-ground cornmeal
¼ cup warm water (105°F to 115°F)	¼ cup flax seeds
⅓ cup honey	1 cup wheat bran (unprocessed)
2 teaspoons salt	1½ cups whole wheat flour
1 egg	About 3 tablespoons sesame seeds

❶ In large bowl, mix starter, milk and 1½ cups of the bread flour. For sourest flavor, cover; let stand in warm place until bubbly and sour smelling, 12 to 24 hours. If time is short, proceed with recipe.

❷ In small bowl, dissolve yeast in water; let stand 5 minutes. Stir into starter mixture with honey, salt, egg, oil, oats, bulgur, cornmeal, flax seeds, wheat bran, 1 cup of the whole wheat flour and 1 cup remaining bread flour to create manageable dough. Turn dough out onto surface dusted with remaining ½ cup whole wheat flour and ½ cup bread flour. Knead 10 minutes (adding more bread flour as needed to prevent sticking, or use a bit of oil on hands and surface) or until dough is smooth and elastic. Place in greased bowl; turn dough greased side up. Cover; let rise in warm place 1½ to 2½ hours or until doubled in size.

❸ Grease 2 large baking sheets. Punch dough down. Knead briefly; divide in half. Shape each half into round loaf, about 6 inches in diameter. Sprinkle sesame seeds on work surface; gently roll dough in seeds, pressing lightly, until all sides are coated. Place each loaf in center of baking sheet. Cover; let rise 30 minutes or until puffy. Heat oven to 375°F. With sharp serrated knife or razor blade, slash tops of loaves with a deep "X." Bake 30 to 35 minutes or until golden brown. Cool on wire racks.

24 servings.
Preparation time: 35 minutes.
Ready to serve: 3 hours, 45 minutes.
Per serving: 200 calories, 3.5 g fat (0.5 g saturated fat), 10 mg cholesterol, 205 mg sodium, 4 g fiber.

$\mathcal{C}$ IABATTA

Italian "slipper bread" is a very light, crusty loaf. Its irregular, flat, flour-dusted shape is described as resembling an old slipper. Its airy texture makes it an excellent option for slicing horizontally and making sandwiches with grilled meat or vegetables.

1	teaspoon active dry yeast		1	teaspoon olive oil
1¼	cups warm water (105°F to 115°F)		1½	teaspoons salt
1	cup *European Sourdough Starter* (page 77)		3	cups unbleached bread flour
1	tablespoon nonfat dry milk			

❶ In large bowl, dissolve yeast in water; let stand 5 minutes. Stir in starter, dry milk, oil and salt; mix well. Stir in flour to form wet, sticky dough. Beat well by hand 5 minutes; dough will become elastic and start to pull away from sides of bowl.

❷ Cover bowl with towel. Let rise in warm place 3 hours or until tripled in size and full of air bubbles. Generously dust 2 large baking sheets with flour. Using sharp knife or dough scraper, cut dough in half in bowl. Scoop out half of dough onto 1 baking sheet. Generously sprinkle with flour. Pull and stretch dough to form 6x12-inch rectangular loaf. Use floured hands to tuck under edges to even shape of loaf. Repeat with remaining dough half.

❸ Let rise in warm place, uncovered, 30 minutes (loaves will spread as well as rise). Heat oven to 425°F, with baking stone on lowest rack of oven, if desired. Bake loaves on baking sheets, or slide onto baking stone, 25 to 30 minutes or until golden brown. Spray inside of oven with water several times during first 10 minutes of baking for crustier loaves. Cool on wire racks.

16 servings.
Preparation time: 25 minutes.
Ready to serve: 4 hours, 50 minutes.
Per serving: 135 calories, 0.5 g fat (0 g saturated fat), 0 mg cholesterol, 220 mg sodium, 1 g fiber.

BAKER'S NOTE

• This dough is very wet and requires a long rising time to achieve its open and tender texture; it should not be over handled.

SUN-DRIED TOMATO BATARDS

Bâtards are oblong loaves of French-style bread, with slashed tops.

1 (¼-oz.) pkg. active dry yeast	2¼ teaspoons salt
2 cups warm water (105°F to 115°F)	1½ teaspoons dried basil
1 cup *European Sourdough Starter* (page 77)	3 garlic cloves, minced
1 cup whole wheat flour	1 cup olive oil-marinated sun-dried tomatoes, drained well, chopped
½ cup rye flour	Cornmeal
3 to 4 cups unbleached bread flour	

❶ In large bowl, dissolve yeast in water; let stand 5 minutes. Stir in starter; mix well.

❷ Stir whole wheat flour, rye flour, 3 cups of the bread flour, salt, basil and garlic into starter mixture; beat until soft dough forms.

❸ Turn dough out onto floured surface. Knead 10 to 15 minutes, adding as much remaining bread flour as needed to make smooth and elastic dough. Place in greased bowl; turn greased side up. Cover; let rise in warm place 1½ to 2 hours or until doubled in size.

❹ Divide dough in half; form into balls. Flatten dough into 1-inch-thick rounds. Spread tomatoes on surface of dough; knead into dough until evenly distributed. Shape each half into oblong loaves with tapered ends; place on cornmeal-dusted baking sheets. Cover; let rise 45 minutes or until nearly doubled in size.

❺ Heat oven to 400°F, with baking stone on lowest oven rack, if desired. With sharp serrated knife or razor blade, make 3 diagonal slashes along tops of loaves. Bake 35 to 40 minutes, spraying loaves with water several times during first 10 minutes of baking, until light golden brown. Cool on wire racks.

24 servings.
Preparation time: 40 minutes.
Ready to serve: 4 hours, 30 minutes.
Per serving: 120 calories, 1 g fat (0 g saturated fat), 0 mg cholesterol, 230 mg sodium, 2 g fiber.

VARIATION Olive-Pine Nut Bâtards
Substitute dried rosemary for basil, and ¼ cup pitted and quartered kalamata olives and ½ cup coarsly toasted pine nuts for the sun-dried tomatoes.

YUKON GOLD POTATO BREAD

Yukon Gold, a popular variety of potato that has a deep golden color, makes a wonderful potato bread. Potato water is great food for bread yeast and sourdough starters, and adding some mashed Yukon Golds to a sourdough creates moist, dense bread that keeps well.

2	large or 3 medium Yukon Gold potatoes	1	cup old-fashioned rolled oats, plus additional for sprinkling loaves
1	cup *Miner's Sourdough Starter* (page 76)	3	tablespoons vegetable oil
2	cups potato water	2	tablespoons molasses or sugar
6½ to 7	cups unbleached bread flour	1	tablespoon salt
			Melted butter

❶ Cut potatoes into quarters. Place in saucepan; cover with about 3 cups water. Bring to a boil; reduce heat and simmer 25 minutes or until very tender. Drain, reserving water. Discard potato skins; mash potatoes with ½ cup of the cooking water (you should have about 2 cups thick potato water); cover and refrigerate.

❷ In large bowl, mix starter, cooled potato water, 4 cups of the flour and 1 cup oats. Cover; let stand at room temperature 18 to 24 hours.

❸ Grease 2 (9x5-inch) loaf pans. Stir oil, molasses and salt into starter mixture; beat vigorously to blend. Beat in mashed potatoes and 2 cups flour until soft dough forms. Turn dough out onto generously floured surface. Knead 6 to 8 minutes, adding more flour as needed, until dough is satiny and smooth. Divide dough in half. Shape into loaves; place in pans. Cover; let rise in warm place 3 hours or until nearly doubled in size.

❹ Heat oven to 375°F. Brush dough with butter; sprinkle with oats. Bake 45 to 50 minutes or until golden brown (tent with foil if crust begins to brown too quickly). Remove from pans; cool on wire rack.

32 servings.
Preparation time: 45 minutes.
Ready to serve: 28 hours, 30 minutes.
Per serving: 160 calories, 2 g fat (0.5 g saturated fat), 0 mg cholesterol, 220 mg sodium, 1.5 g fiber.

BAKER'S NOTE
• To vary the taste of this great bread, try substituting 1 cup cornmeal or ⅔ cup wheat germ for rolled oats.

GOLD RUSH SOURDOUGH BREAD

The distinctly-flavored traditional San Francisco-style sourdough bread is very hard to recreate at home, primarily because the wild yeasts from the area are unique. However, it's still possible to create wonderful sourdough bread — with thick chewy crust and a dense, sour crumb — with your own starter.

18 HOURS BEFORE USE

1 cup *Miner's Sourdough Starter* (page 76)

1½ cups warm water (105°F to 115°F)

4 cups unbleached bread flour

2 teaspoons sugar

2 teaspoons salt

BAKING DAY

2 cups unbleached bread flour

Cornmeal

❶ About 18 hours before you bake, in large bowl, mix starter, water, 4 cups flour, sugar and salt until well blended. Cover with plastic wrap; let stand at room temperature.

❷ On baking day, stir 1 cup of the flour into sourdough mixture. Turn dough out onto floured surface. Knead 8 to 10 minutes, adding as much remaining 1 cup flour as needed to make smooth and elastic dough. Divide dough in half. Shape into 2 loaves, 15- to 18-inches long. Place in French baguette pans or on cornmeal-dusted baking sheets. Cover with damp kitchen towel; let rise in warm place 2 hours or until doubled in size.

❸ Heat oven to 400°F, with roasting pan half-filled with hot water on bottom rack. With sharp serrated knife or razor blade, make 3 diagonal slashes along tops of loaves; lightly spray with water. Bake 45 minutes or until golden brown. Cool on wire rack.

24 servings.

Preparation time: 40 minutes.

Ready to serve: 22 hours, 30 minutes.

Per serving: 145 calories, 0 g fat (0 g saturated fat), 0 mg cholesterol, 195 mg sodium, 1 g fiber.

VARIATION Wholewheat Sourdough Bread

Substitute 3 cups whole wheat flour for 3 cups of the bread flour at the beginning of recipe.

VARIATION Sourdough Petit Pain (Hard Rolls)

Divide dough into 12 equal pieces. Shape into oblong rolls; let rise as directed. Make long horizontal slash along top of each roll before baking. Spray inside of oven with water several times during first 10 minutes of baking for crustier rolls.

$\mathcal{M}$INI BREADS

Individually fresh-baked breads, from buttery dinner rolls to chewy bagels, seem to be forever popular. Try your hand at shaping long, crisp breadsticks or twisting a grainy dough into thick, soft pretzels perfect for whimsical sandwiches-to-go. Hot, steamy popovers and pillowy steamed buns filled with sesame and honey push the definitions of classic baking and pull in many global bread traditions.

Giant Soft Pretzels, page 101

$\mathcal{A}$LL-AMERICAN DINNER PARTY ROLLS

When I think about dinner rolls, I think of suburban America in the 1950's. The creative ways of shaping dinner rolls, and their fanciful names, automatically elevate any occasion (see sidebar on page 95).

1	(¼-oz.) pkg. active dry yeast
¼	cup warm water (105°F to 115°F)
¾	cup warm milk (105°F to 115°F)
¼	cup sugar
1	teaspoon salt
1	egg
¼	cup butter or margarine, softened
2	cups unbleached all-purpose flour
¼	cup toasted wheat germ
1¼ to 1½	cups whole wheat flour

❶ In large bowl, dissolve yeast in water. Stir in milk, sugar, salt, egg, butter, all-purpose flour and wheat germ. Beat until smooth (with wooden spoon or mixer). Stir in enough of the whole wheat flour to make dough easy to handle. Turn dough out onto lightly floured surface. Knead 6 minutes or until smooth and elastic. Place in greased bowl; turn dough greased side up. Cover; let rise in warm place 1½ to 2 hours or until doubled in size.

❷ Punch dough down. Shape as desired. Place rolls on greased baking sheets or in muffin cups; let rise 20 to 30 minutes or until puffy. Heat oven to 400°F. Bake 15 to 20 minutes or until golden brown.

24 servings.
Preparation time: 40 minutes.
Ready to serve: 3 hours, 25 minutes.

Per serving: 95 calories, 2.5 g total fat (1.5 g saturated fat), 15 mg cholesterol, 115 mg sodium, 1.5 g fiber.

VARIATION Herbed Potato Rolls

In large bowl, combine warm water (potato water is good if you are cooking the potato from scratch) and milk. Beat in ½ cup warm mashed potato, 1 tablespoon Dijon mustard and ½ teaspoon dried thyme. Stir in yeast and 2 tablespoons honey (omit sugar). Let stand 5 minutes. Beat in salt, egg, butter and 3½ to 4 cups all-purpose flour. Proceed as directed. Dust rolls with flour before baking.

BAKER'S NOTES
- Brush rolls with milk before baking, or butter afterwards for a tender, browned finish. Dust rolls with freshly grated Parmesan cheese, kosher (coarse) salt, herbs or seeds before baking for added flavor.
- This dough could be made in a large-capacity bread machine, so it would be ready to shape and bake just before serving, saving time during entertaining preparation but still allowing you to treat your guests to home-baked bread.

DINNER ROLE SHAPES

Here are some creative ways to shape your dinner rolls. While the recipe is grand, a little variety always adds interest ... and can start some conversation. Here's how to produce some intriguing shapes.

• **Traditional Dinner Rolls:** Place 2 (1½-inch) balls in 24 greased muffin cups.

• **Cloverleaf:** Place 3 (1-inch) balls in 24 greased muffin cups.

• **Fan Tans:** Roll half of dough into a 13x9-inch rectangle. Spread with softened butter. Cut lengthwise into 6 (1½-inches-wide) strips. Stack strips evenly, one on top of the other; cut into 12 (1-inch-wide) pieces. Place cut sides down in 12 greased muffin cups. Brush rolls with butter.

• **Crescents:** Roll half of dough into a 12-inch circle. Spread with softened butter. Cut into 16 wedges. Roll up, beginning at round edge. Place on greased baking sheets, point side down; curve rolls slightly.

Coil

Twist

Crescent

• **Figure 8's:** Using half of the dough, roll into a 12-inch square. Spread with softened butter. Fold square in half. Cut into 24 strips, about ½-inch wide and 6-inches long. Twist each strip into a figure 8 shape. Place on greased baking sheets.

• **French or Bow Knots:** Repeat process for Figure 8's, but tie loose knot in one end of strip; pull longer end of strip through center of knot.

• **Twists:** Divide dough into 18 equal pieces. Roll each piece into a 12-inch rope; fold in half and twist.

• **Coils:** Repeat process for twists, but form each rope into a coil, tucking end under.

PESTO SNAIL ROLLS

Yet another rebirth of the dinner roll, these spiraled breads are a savory take on cinnamon rolls. Prepared basil pesto is an easy spread to have on hand to fill this tender, rich dough.

2	(¼-oz.) pkg. active dry yeast	5½ to 6	cups unbleached all-purpose flour
1	tablespoon sugar	6	egg yolks
¾	cup warm water (105°F to 115°F)	1	cup (4 oz.) freshly grated Romano cheese
1	cup milk	¾	cup fresh (soft) goat cheese
⅓	cup butter or margarine	¼	cup prepared basil pesto
1	teaspoon salt		

❶ In small bowl, dissolve yeast and sugar in water; let stand 15 minutes or until foamy. In medium saucepan or microwave, heat milk, butter and salt to 120°F to 130°F. In large bowl, combine 2 cups of the flour, egg yolks, warm milk mixture and yeast mixture. Beat with electric mixer at low speed 30 seconds, scraping down sides of bowl. Increase speed to high, beating 3 minutes. Stir in Romano cheese and as much flour as possible (about 3½ cups) with wooden spoon. Turn dough out onto lightly floured surface. Knead in enough remaining flour 6 to 8 minutes, to create moderately stiff dough that is smooth and elastic. Place in greased bowl; turn dough greased side up. Cover; let rise in warm place 45 to 60 minutes or until doubled in size.

❷ Punch dough down; turn out onto lightly floured surface. Divide dough in half. Let rest 10 minutes. Grease 2 large baking sheets or 2 (13x9-inch) pans.

❸ In small bowl, mix goat cheese and pesto. Roll half of dough into 12x10-inch rectangle. Spread with half of pesto mixture. Roll up jelly-roll fashion starting with short end. Cut into 10 (1-inch-thick) slices with sharp knife or dental floss (see Baker's notes, page 113). Place rolls on baking sheets or in pans. Repeat with remaining dough and pesto. Cover; let rise in warm place 20 to 30 minutes or until nearly doubled in size. Heat oven to 350°F. Bake 20 to 25 minutes or until golden brown. Serve warm.

20 servings.
Preparation time: 2 hours, 15 minutes.
Ready to serve: 2 hours, 55 minutes.
Per serving: 230 calories, 9.5 g total fat (4.5 g saturated fat), 85 mg cholesterol, 225 mg sodium, 1 g fiber.

VARIATION   Butterfly Rolls

If baking on baking sheets, snip each roll twice with kitchen shears or knife (on opposite sides), about 1 inch in toward center. Replace Romano with shredded fontina and use 1 cup soft goat cheese and 2 teaspoons crushed *herbes de Provence* to fill rolls.

CHEWY CORNMEAL SAGE TWISTS

These soft and chewy breadsticks are great dipped in flavored olive oil or salsas.
Serve them with summer salads or hot winter soups.

1 (¼-oz.) pkg. active dry yeast	2 tablespoons chopped fresh sage or 1½ teaspoons crumbled dried
1 teaspoon honey	1½ teaspoons salt
1¼ cups warm water (105°F to 115°F)	1¾ cups unbleached all-purpose flour
2 tablespoons olive oil, plus additional for brushing breadsticks	2½ to 3 cups yellow cornmeal, plus additional for dusting breadsticks

1 In large bowl, dissolve yeast and honey in water; let stand 5 minutes.

2 Stir in 2 tablespoons oil, sage and salt. Stir in flour with wooden spoon. Gradually stir in 2½ cups of the cornmeal, stirring until soft dough forms. Turn dough out onto surface dusted with remaining ½ cup cornmeal. Knead dough, working in cornmeal as needed, 10 minutes or until dough is firm and elastic.

3 Place dough in greased bowl; turn dough greased side up. Cover; let rise in warm place 1 hour or until nearly doubled in size.

4 Heat oven to 400°F, positioning oven racks in center and upper third of oven. Grease 3 baking sheets or line with parchment paper. Divide dough into 4 equal pieces. Roll each piece into ¼-inch-thick rectangle, about 8x6 inches. Cut dough into 1-inch strips. Twist each strip into corkscrew; place on baking sheets.

5 Brush breadsticks with oil; dust lightly with cornmeal. Bake 15 to 20 minutes or until golden brown. Cool on wire racks.

32 servings.
Preparation time: 50 minutes.
Ready to serve: 2 hours, 25 minutes.
Per serving: 85 calories, 1.5 g total fat (0 g saturated fat), 0 mg cholesterol, 110 mg sodium, 1 g fiber.

BAKER'S NOTE

• Because this recipe makes a large number of breadsticks, you can freeze part of them for another occasion. After baking, let them cool and then lay them out in single layer on a baking sheet; cover and freeze until solid. They can then be transferred to a plastic freezer bag so they take up less room. Freeze up to three months. Thaw at room temperature or place frozen breadsticks on a baking sheet in a 300°F oven 15 minutes or until just warm.

ITALIAN GRISSINS

Long, skinny and very crunchy breadsticks (often offered in paper wrappers) are a staple on Italian trattoria tables. Homemade, they are wonderfully flavorful, charmingly crafted in appearance ... and they keep nearly as well as commercially made ones.

1	(¼-oz.) pkg. active dry yeast or 2¼ teaspoons bread machine yeast
3 to 3⅓	cups unbleached all-purpose or bread flour
¾	cup freshly grated Parmesan cheese
6	garlic cloves, minced
1	teaspoon each salt, freshly ground pepper
1	cup plus 2 tablespoons water
1	tablespoon olive oil
1	egg white beaten with 1 tablespoon water

❶ Place yeast, flour, ½ cup of the Parmesan, garlic, salt, pepper, water and oil in 1½-lb. loaf bread machine, following manufacturer's directions. Select Dough cycle; press Start. Remove dough to lightly floured surface and punch down (knead in a little more flour if dough seems sticky). Divide dough in half (keep 1 half in refrigerator while shaping first half). Roll each piece into 12x12x¼-inch square. Cover with plastic wrap; let rest 10 minutes. Cut each square into 24 (½-inch-wide) strips. Line 4 baking sheets with parchment paper. Roll each strip between palms of your hands into pencil-thin ropes.

❷ Arrange breadsticks on baking sheet, sides not touching. Cover; let rise about 20 minutes. Heat oven to 375°F. Just before baking, brush breadsticks with egg white mixture and sprinkle with remaining ¼ cup Parmesan. Bake 16 to 18 minutes or until golden brown. Cool completely on wire rack. Store airtight.

48 servings.
Preparation time: 2 hours, 30 minutes.
Ready to serve: 3 hours.
Per serving: 40 calories, 1 g total fat (0.5 g saturated fat), 1 mg cholesterol, 80 mg sodium, 0.5 g fiber.

BAKER'S NOTES

• For more visual interest and flavor variety, consider using a peppercorn mixture for the freshly ground pepper. Mixtures usually include black, white, pink and green peppercorns; each has its own unique flavor and spiciness.

• If each half of the dough is cut into 12 strips (instead of 24), these breadsticks become very long, and are fun for entertaining. Makes two dozen breadsticks.

STEAMED ASIAN HONEY BUNS

These buns are steamed rather than baked and they have no crust. These are similar to the dough used for Chinese barbecued pork bao *(buns). Serve with any Asian meal, alongside a main dish salad or for a breakfast or snack.*

1	(¼-oz.) pkg. active dry yeast
1	tablespoon honey
2	tablespoons warm water (105°F to 115°F)
1	cup warm milk (105°F to 115°F)
¼	teaspoon salt
3 to 3½	cups unbleached all-purpose flour
½	cup sesame seeds
6	tablespoons honey

❶ In large bowl, dissolve yeast and 1 tablespoon honey in warm water. Let stand 5 minutes or until foamy. Stir in milk, salt and enough flour to create stiff dough that is easy to handle.

❷ Turn dough out onto lightly floured surface. Knead 4 minutes or until smooth and elastic. Place in greased bowl; turn dough greased side up. Cover; let rise in warm place 1½ to 2 hours or until doubled in size. Meanwhile, combine sesame seeds and 6 tablespoons honey; set aside.

❸ Punch down dough; divide into 20 pieces. Roll or pat each piece into 3½-inch circle. Place 2 teaspoons honey filling in center of circle. Bring edge up around filling; twist to seal. Place on 3-inch square of waxed paper. Repeat with remaining circles. Cover; let rise in warm place 30 minutes.

❹ Place 5 to 6 buns on heatproof plate on rack in deep kettle, steamer or wok. Cover; steam over boiling water 12 minutes or until puffed and slightly firm to the touch. Repeat with remaining buns. Add water to kettle as necessary. Once steamed, immediately remove waxed paper squares from buns.

20 servings.
Preparation time: 35 minutes.
Ready to serve: 4 hours.
Per serving: 115 calories, 2 g total fat (0.5 g saturated fat), 0 mg cholesterol, 35 mg sodium, 1 g fiber.

VARIATION   Ginger Honey Buns
Add 2 teaspoons grated fresh ginger to sesame-honey filling.

CARAMELIZED ONION BURGER BUNS

Who needs those flavorless, soft, commercially-made burger buns that stick to the roof of your mouth? Before a summer grilling bash, take some time to try your hand at freshly baked buns. You can even freeze unused ones until you need them again.

¼	cup butter or margarine
1½	cups chopped onion
3	tablespoons sugar
1	(¼-oz.) pkg. active dry yeast
1½	cups warm water (105°F to 115°F)
½	cup warm milk (105°F to 115°F)
2	teaspoons salt
5 to 5½	cups unbleached all-purpose flour
1	egg beaten with 1 tablespoon water
	Freshly ground pepper

❶ In medium skillet melt butter over medium heat. Add onion and 1 tablespoon of the sugar; cook and stir over medium heat 12 to 15 minutes or until golden brown. Cool.

❷ Meanwhile, in large bowl, dissolve yeast and remaining 2 tablespoons sugar in water. Add milk, salt and 3 cups of the flour. Beat at medium speed, scraping bowl often, 1 to 2 minutes or until smooth. By hand, stir in half of onion mixture and enough remaining flour to make dough easy to handle. Turn dough out onto lightly floured surface. Knead 5 minutes or until smooth and elastic. Place in greased bowl; turn dough greased side up. Cover; let rise in warm place 1 hour or until nearly doubled in size.

❸ Punch down dough; divide in half. With floured hands shape each half into 6 rounds; place on greased baking sheets. Flatten each to 3½- to 4-inch round. Cover; let rise 30 minutes or until nearly doubled in size. Heat oven to 400°F. Brush dough rounds with egg mixture, evenly top with remaining onion mixture; sprinkle with pepper. Bake 15 to 18 minutes or until golden brown. Cool completely on wire rack.

12 servings.
Preparation time: 4 hours.
Ready to serve: 2 hours, 10 minutes.
Per serving: 255 calories, 5 g total fat (2.5 g saturated fat), 25 mg cholesterol, 425 mg sodium, 2 g fiber.

GIANT SOFT PRETZELS

The name for pretzel is derived from the German brezel *or little arms. Culinary history tells a story from the early Christian church — the twisted dough represented arms crossed across the chest in prayer.*

- ⅓ cup bulgur (cracked wheat)
- ⅔ cup boiling water
- 3 to 3½ cups unbleached all-purpose flour
- 1 (¼-oz.) pkg. active dry yeast
- 1 teaspoon garlic salt
- 1 teaspoon poppy seeds, plus more for sprinkling if desired
- 1¼ cups very warm water (120°F to 130°F)
  Kosher (coarse) salt

❶ In small bowl, cover bulgur with boiling water; let stand 30 minutes. Drain any excess water.

❷ In food processor fitted with plastic dough blade or metal blade, combine 3 cups of the flour, bulgur, yeast, garlic salt and 1 teaspoon poppy seeds. With motor running, slowly pour warm water through feed tube, mixing until dough forms and clears side of bowl (if dough is sticky, add a little more flour). Process until dough turns around bowl 25 times. Turn dough onto lightly floured surface. Shape into a ball; cover with inverted bowl and let rest 10 minutes. Generously grease 2 large baking sheets.

❸ Divide dough into 12 equal pieces. Shape each piece into 20-inch rope. To shape into pretzels, curve ends of each rope to make a circle; cross ends at top. Twist ends once and lay over bottom of circle. Place on baking sheets. Cover; let pretzels rise 30 minutes or until nearly doubled in size.

❹ Heat oven to 400°F. Brush pretzels lightly with water and sprinkle with kosher salt and poppy seeds. Bake 20 to 25 minutes or until golden brown. Cool on wire racks.

12 servings.
Preparation time: 1 hour, 45 minutes.
Ready to serve: 2 hours, 22 minutes.
Per serving: 130 calories, 0.5 g total fat (0 g saturated fat), 0 mg cholesterol, 275 mg sodium, 2 g fiber.

NGEL BISCUITS

I've always liked the name of these biscuits — and the idea of adding yeast to a biscuit seems like a great idea to me. The name implies they are otherworldly light in texture, and that they are! The addition of sour cream gives a slight tang to the crumb, and these biscuits are heavenly with a smidge of butter and jam.

3½	cups all-purpose flour
2	tablespoons sugar
½	teaspoon baking powder
½	teaspoon baking soda
½	teaspoon salt
¼	cup butter or margarine
1	(¼-oz.) pkg. active dry yeast
¼	cup warm water (105°F to 115°F)
1	cup dairy sour cream
½	cup warm milk

❶ In large bowl, combine flour, sugar, baking powder, baking soda and salt. Cut butter into dry ingredients with pastry blender or fork until mixture resembles coarse crumbs; set aside.

❷ In small bowl, dissolve yeast in warm water. Stir into dry ingredients with sour cream and milk; blend well.

❸ Turn dough out onto lightly floured surface. Knead 10 to 15 times; form into a ball. Pat or roll dough to ½-inch thickness. Cut with 2½- to 3-inch round cutters. Place biscuits on ungreased baking sheet.

❹ Cover; let rise in warm place 45 minutes or until doubled in size.

❺ Heat oven to 400°F. Bake biscuits 15 minutes or until golden brown. Serve warm.

15 servings.
Preparation time: 15 minutes.
Ready to serve: 1 hour, 15 minutes.
Per serving: 175 calories, 6.5 g total fat (4 g saturated fat), 20 mg cholesterol, 165 mg sodium, 1 g fiber.

SAVORY SKY-HIGH POPOVERS

Popovers are found in many guises — from individual rolls that break open and are spread with butter, to larger ones that become a bowl for salads. They can even be made sweet and filled with sautéed apples (otherwise know as Dutch Babies). The British favorite, Yorkshire Pudding, is another version of this egg batter bread.

2   eggs
½   cup unbleached all-purpose flour
½   cup whole wheat flour
1   cup chicken broth
½   teaspoon salt

❶ Heat oven to 450°F. Generously grease 6-cup popover pan or 6 (6-oz.) custard cups.

❷ In medium bowl, lightly whisk eggs. Beat in all-purpose flour, whole wheat flour, broth and salt just until smooth. Fill cups about half full. Bake 20 minutes. Decrease oven temperature to 350°F; bake 20 minutes longer or until deep golden brown.

❸ Immediately remove popovers from cups and serve hot.

6 servings.
Preparation time: 10 minutes.
Ready to serve: 50 minutes.
Per serving: 105 calories, 2 g total fat (0.5 g saturated fat), 70 mg cholesterol, 390 mg sodium, 1.5 g fiber.

VARIATION   Herbed Savory Popovers
Stir in ½ teaspoon dried *fines herbes* to popover batter.

CRUSTY DAKOTA HEARTH ROLLS

Rustic, crusty rolls like these keep well and are a good choice to serve with one-dish meals. Full of prairie harvest goodness, they showcase some of the best natural ingredients grown in the Midwest.

2 (¼-oz.) pkg. active dry yeast	2½ cups whole wheat flour
2 tablespoons packed brown sugar	2 to 2½ cups unbleached all-purpose or bread flour
2¼ cups warm water (105°F to 115°F)	½ cup coarsely chopped hulled pumpkin seeds
1½ cups cooked wild rice or wheat berries	¼ cup unsalted sunflower seeds
1 tablespoon salt	2 tablespoons whole grain millet Cornmeal

❶ In large bowl, dissolve yeast and sugar in ½ cup of the water; let stand 5 minutes. Stir in remaining 1¾ cups water, wild rice, salt and whole wheat flour, beating with wooden spoon until smooth. Add 1 cup of the all-purpose flour, beating again until smooth. Gradually stir in remaining all-purpose flour until soft dough is formed that just clears side of bowl.

❷ Turn dough out onto lightly floured surface. Knead 2 minutes or until smooth and elastic. Flatten dough with hands; sprinkle with pumpkin seeds, sunflower seeds and millet. Fold dough over; knead gently until ingredients are incorporated into dough. Place in greased bowl; turn dough greased side up and dust with a little flour. Cover; let rise in warm place 1 to 1½ hours or until doubled in size.

❸ Sprinkle 2 large baking sheets with cornmeal. Punch dough down. Turn dough out onto lightly floured surface; divide into 4 pieces. Divide each piece into 5 equal portions, making 20 pieces of dough. Shape into round balls; press to flatten slightly. Place on baking sheets, 1 inch apart. Cover; let rise in warm place 30 to 40 minutes or until nearly doubled in size.

❹ Heat oven to 400°F, with baking stone on bottom oven rack, if desired. Snip around edge of each roll 4 or 5 times, cutting nearly to center with kitchen shears; lightly dust tops with flour. Bake on baking sheets or baking stone (bake on lower and upper racks, switching positions halfway through baking) 18 to 22 minutes or until lightly browned around edges. Serve warm.

20 servings.
Preparation time: 45 minutes.
Ready to serve: 3 hours, 5 minutes.
Per serving: 150 calories, 3 g total fat (0.5 g saturated fat), 0 mg cholesterol, 415 mg sodium, 3 g fiber.

ELI "EVERYTHING" BAGELS

Bagels have garnered a stardom outside of their traditional ethnic roots like no other bread — they've become ubiquitous, found in every grocery store bakery and in numerous street corner bagel shops. Sadly, many are large, bready and soft-crusted. This is NOT the definition of a true New York-style Jewish bagel — which is crusty outside and boasts a thick and chewy texture inside. The unique feature of this mini bread is in the preparation for baking: Rings of dough are quickly boiled in water to create the characteristic sheen on the crust. I have a favorite bagel source (a Jewish mother) who tells me that using potato water is the best for bagels — try it and see! "Everything" bagels contain white, whole wheat and rye flours, and are topped with sesame and poppy seeds and finely minced onion.

2	(¼-oz.) pkg. active dry yeast
2	tablespoons honey
2	cups warm water or potato water (105°F to 115°F)
1½	teaspoons salt
2	eggs
2	cups whole wheat flour
½	cup rye flour
3 to 4	cups unbleached bread flour
1	tablespoon sugar or malted barley syrup
1	teaspoon baking soda
¼	cup unhulled or hulled sesame seeds
¼	cup poppy seeds
2	tablespoons dried minced onions

❶ In large bowl, dissolve yeast and honey in water; let stand 5 minutes. Beat in salt, eggs, whole wheat flour and rye flour with wooden spoon. Gradually beat in enough of the bread flour (about 3 cups) to make stiff dough.

❷ Turn dough out onto floured surface. Knead 10 minutes or until smooth and elastic, working in as much flour as needed. Place dough in greased bowl; turn dough greased side up. Cover; let rise 45 minutes or until puffy.

❸ Punch dough down; divide into 12 equal pieces. To shape, knead 1 piece at a time into a smooth ball. Gently flatten each ball slightly and press through center with thumbs to make a hole. With thumbs in hole, pull dough gently to shape an evenly thick ring, 3½-inches wide. Place formed dough on lightly floured surface; cover with plastic wrap and let rise 20 to 25 minutes or until puffy.

❹ Bring 2 quarts water to a boil; add sugar and baking soda. Adjust heat to maintain a gentle boil. Lay cloth dish towel on surface near boiling water for draining bagels. Grease 2 large baking sheets. On plate, mix sesame seeds, poppy seeds and minced onion.

❺ Drop bagels into boiling water, up to 4 at a time. As they rise to the surface, turn them over and cook 1 minute longer. Lift from water with slotted spoon or wide spatula; drain briefly on dish towel. Lay bagels on seed mixture to coat; turn over and coat other side (or just sprinkle seed mixture on top). Transfer to baking sheet.

❻ Heat oven to 400°F. Bake 30 to 35 minutes or until golden brown, switching baking sheet positions halfway through baking. Cool on wire racks.

12 servings.

Preparation time: 1 hour, 20 minutes.

Ready to serve: 1 hour, 50 minutes.

Per serving: 270 calories, 4.5 g total fat (0.5 g saturated fat), 35 mg cholesterol, 410 mg sodium, 5 g fiber.

VARIATION Bagel Sticks

Form the 12 pieces of dough into thick rods. Let rise, boil, coat and bake as directed.

BAKER'S NOTES

- If you have time, try a long, slow cool rise in refrigerator after bagels are formed. This fermentation time really develops the flavor of the bread.

- Malted barley syrup is a less dense, less sweet natural sweetener. The flavor is somewhat like blackstrap molasses. It's used for creating a glazed crust on baked goods and is available in natural food stores or co-op groceries. Store it in a glass or plastic container in a cool, dark place. If kept longer than a year, it may ferment (this is what is combined with hops and fermented with yeast to make beer!). If it does become bubbly, refrigerate and use quickly, or discard.

SWEET BREADS & COFFEE CAKES

Here they are — the sweet treats that can't be ignored! Gooey caramel rolls, yeasty tender coffee cakes filled with dried fruits and nuts, breakfast Danish and sweet biscuits with fresh berries and chocolate gravy! Savor these over coffee with friends, share them with your office mates, or serve them at a spectacular family birthday brunch — there will be no leftovers for the freezer!

Apricot Almond Tea Twist, page 116

109

$\mathcal{D}$ORIS' BOHEMIAN POPPY SEED BUNS

Czech-American bakers have passed on a legacy of mild sweet yeast pastries that are loved in many parts of the U.S. This one is adapted from a generous baker's original.

BUNS
1	recipe *Sweet Yeast Dough* (page 37)
½	cup poppy seeds
½	cup half-and-half
¼	cup honey
2	teaspoons grated lemon peel
1	egg, beaten

LEMON DRIZZLE
1½	cups powdered sugar
2	tablespoons lemon juice
2	teaspoons grated lemon peel

❶ Prepare dough as directed up through first rise.

❷ Meanwhile, prepare filling: Place poppy seeds in blender; process until just ground. In medium saucepan, combine ground poppy seeds, half-and-half and honey. Cook over medium-low heat 10 to 12 minutes or until thickened. Stir in 2 teaspoons lemon peel; cool.

❸ Grease 2 (13x9-inch) baking pans. Divide dough into 24 equal pieces; form into balls. Flatten each ball into 4½-inch round. Place 2 teaspoons poppy seed filling in center. Fold dough up and over filling, pressing edges together to seal filling inside. Place filled buns, seam side down, in pan. Cover; let rise 30 to 45 minutes or until puffy.

❹ Heat oven to 350°F. Brush dough with egg. Bake 13 to 18 minutes or until golden brown. Cool on wire rack.

❺ In medium bowl, mix powdered sugar, lemon juice and 2 teaspoons lemon peel until smooth. Drizzle over buns.

24 servings.
Preparation time: 1 hour, 30 minutes.
Ready to serve: 4 hours, 5 minutes.

Per serving: 220 calories, 5.5 g fat (2.5 g saturated fat), 35 mg cholesterol, 130 mg sodium, 1.5 g fiber.

BAKER'S NOTES

- The miniscule slate blue seeds of the poppy have a long culinary tradition, especially in Central European, Slavic, Balkan and Middle Eastern cooking. Store them tightly covered in a cool, dark cupboard as they become rancid easily.

- One-half to ⅔ cup canned poppy seed filling can be substituted for the from-scratch filling.

CASHEW CARAMEL ROLLS

Who can resist sticky buns? The ooey-gooier the better! Use dark brown sugar for a deeper caramel flavor.

1¼ cups packed dark brown sugar
½ cup butter or margarine
¼ cup honey or dark corn syrup
2 tablespoons golden rum or 1 teaspoon rum extract, if desired

1½ cups chopped salted cashews
½ recipe *Sweet Yeast Dough* (page 37)
2 tablespoons butter or margarine, softened

❶ In medium saucepan, heat 1 cup of the brown sugar and ½ cup butter. Heat to boiling, stirring constantly; remove from heat. Stir in honey and rum. Pour into 13x9-inch pan. Sprinkle with 1 cup of the cashews.

❷ Prepare dough as directed. After first rising, punch dough down. Turn out onto lightly floured surface. Roll dough into 15x10-inch rectangle. Spread with 2 tablespoons softened butter. Sprinkle with remaining ½ cup cashews and ¼ cup brown sugar. Roll up jelly-roll fashion, starting at long edge. Pinch edge of dough into roll to seal. Stretch and shape until even. Using dental floss or strong thread (see Baker's Notes.), cut roll into 12 slices. Place slices in pan. Cover; let rise 45 minutes or until doubled in size.

❸ Heat oven to 350°F. Bake 30 to 35 minutes or until golden brown, tenting with foil if tops begin to brown too quickly. Immediately invert pan onto heatproof tray, foil-lined baking sheet or serving plate. Let stand 1 minute so caramel will drizzle down; remove pan.

15 servings.
Preparation time: 1 hour, 30 minutes.
Ready to serve: 4 hours.
Per serving: 360 calories, 17 g fat (7.5 g saturated fat), 40 mg cholesterol, 245 mg sodium, 1.5 g fiber.

BAKER'S NOTES

- To make these rolls ahead of time, prepare them up to the point of slicing and putting them in pan. They can then be covered and refrigerated up to 48 hours or frozen up to four weeks. If refrigerated, bake right out of the refrigerator. If frozen, thaw at room temperature 1 to 2 hours, then let rise 1½ hours. Bake as directed.

- Slicing rolled dough is easier using a length of dental floss, fishing line or strong thread. Just lay floss under rolled dough, bring up ends, cross them and pull through dough. The slices keep their shape and are very even.

SPICE ISLES CINNAMON ROLLS

The sweet smell of spices fills the house when these rolls are baking.

½ recipe *Sweet Yeast Dough* (page 37)
½ cup packed brown sugar
1 teaspoon ground cinnamon
½ teaspoon each ground ginger, cardamom, nutmeg

¼ teaspoon ground cloves
2 tablespoons butter or margarine, softened
½ cup golden raisins, if desired
1 recipe *Vanilla Glaze* (page 41)

❶ Prepare dough as directed. Grease 2 large baking sheets. In small bowl, mix brown sugar, cinnamon, ginger, cardamom, nutmeg and cloves together; set aside. After first rise, punch dough down; turn out onto lightly floured surface. Roll into 15x10-inch rectangle. Spread dough with butter. Sprinkle with spice-sugar mixture and raisins; roll up jelly-roll fashion from long side; seal seam well. Using dental floss or strong thread, cut dough into 12 slices. Place slices ½ to 1 inch apart on baking sheets. Cover; let rise in warm place 45 minutes or until doubled in size.

❷ Heat oven to 350°F. Bake 20 to 25 minutes or until golden brown and bubbly. Remove from pan; cool on wire rack. Drizzle with glaze.

12 servings.
Preparation time: 50 minutes.
Ready to serve: 3 hours, 45 minutes.
Per serving: 270 calories, 5.5 g fat (3 g saturated fat), 30 mg cholesterol, 145 mg sodium, 1.5 g fiber.

VARIATIONS Sugar-Crusted Elephant Ears Line 2 large baking sheets with parchment paper. Roll dough out on sugared surface into 18x10-inch rectangle. Brush with 2 tablespoons melted butter; sprinkle with 3 tablespoons sugar and 2 teaspoons ground cinnamon. Roll both short ends toward middle of dough, meeting in center. Cut with dental floss into ⅜-inch slices; coat both sides of slices in sugar. Place 2 inches apart on baking sheets. Let rise 30 minutes. Bake in 375°F oven 15 minutes or until light golden brown.

CITRUS GROVE COBBLESTONE BREAD

Use your bread machine to make this easy light dough, flavored with orange, lemon and lime peel and sugar.

2½ teaspoons bread machine yeast
2 cups unbleached bread flour
2 cups whole wheat flour
¼ cup butter, softened
1 teaspoon salt
1 cup milk
¼ cup orange juice
¼ cup honey
1 egg, lightly beaten
¾ cup sugar

1 tablespoon grated orange peel
2 teaspoons grated lime peel
1 teaspoon grated lemon peel
½ cup butter, melted

CITRUS GLAZE

¼ cup sugar
¼ cup dairy sour cream
2 tablespoons butter
2 teaspoons grated orange peel

❶ Place yeast, bread flour, whole wheat flour, softened butter, salt, milk, orange juice, honey and egg in 1½-lb. loaf bread machine, following manufacturer's instructions. Select Dough cycle; press Start.

❷ Remove dough from machine when cycle is complete. Knead dough on lightly floured surface about 1 minute; cover and let rest 15 minutes. In small bowl, mix ¾ cup sugar, 1 tablespoon orange peel, lime peel and lemon peel. Place melted butter in second bowl. Grease 10-inch tube or 12-cup Bundt pan.

❸ Divide dough into 24 equal pieces, shaping each into a ball. Dip each ball in melted butter; roll in citrus peel-sugar mixture. Place balls in bottom of pan. Cover; let rise 45 minutes or until doubled in size.

❹ Heat oven to 350°F. Bake 20 to 25 minutes or until golden brown. Cool in pan 5 minutes; remove to wire rack. Cool 15 minutes.

❺ Meanwhile, prepare glaze: In medium saucepan stir together ¼ cup sugar, sour cream, 2 tablespoons butter and 2 teaspoons orange peel. Bring to a boil; cook 4 to 5 minutes. Cool 2 to 3 minutes. Drizzle glaze over warm bread.

16 servings.
Preparation time: 45 minutes.
Ready to serve: 3 hours, 20 minutes.
Per serving: 290 calories, 12 g fat (7 g saturated fat), 45 mg cholesterol, 225 mg sodium, 2.5 g fiber.

CHOCOLATE CHERRY CORDIAL BREAD

In Italy, this dramatically dark and not overly sweet chocolate bread is served for celebrations. In the U.S. it has become a popular breakfast bread, an appetizer when spread with mascarpone cheese, or a simple dessert with coffee.

1	cup dried sour cherries	1	tablespoon vanilla
⅓	cup boiling water	2	tablespoons butter, softened
2	tablespoons brandy or orange-flavored liqueur	1	teaspoon salt
1	cup milk	3¾ to 4¼	cups unbleached all-purpose flour
½	cup water	2	oz. semisweet chocolate chips or ½ cup chopped honey-roasted peanuts
1	(¼-oz.) pkg. active dry yeast		
½	cup sugar	1	egg beaten with 1 tablespoon water
⅓	cup Dutch-process cocoa		

❶ In small bowl, combine cherries, boiling water and brandy. Let stand 15 minutes; drain well. In small saucepan, heat milk and ½ cup water just until warm (105°F to 115°F). Pour into large bowl; dissolve yeast in warm liquid; let stand 5 minutes. Stir in sugar, cocoa, vanilla, butter, salt and 2 cups of the flour; beat vigorously. Stir in enough remaining flour to make dough that can be handled.

❷ Turn dough out onto lightly floured surface. Knead 2 minutes. Cover; let rest 15 minutes. Knead in enough flour to keep from sticking 6 to 8 minutes or until smooth and elastic. Knead in cherries and peanuts; if some fall out, just push back in. Place in greased bowl; turn dough greased side up. Cover; let rise in warm place 1½ hours or until doubled in size.

❸ Grease large baking sheet. Punch dough down; turn out onto lightly floured surface. Divide in half and shape into 2 rounds; place on baking sheet. Cover; let rise 45 to 60 minutes or until nearly doubled in size.

❹ Heat oven to 350°F. With sharp serrated knife or razor blade, slash tops of dough; brush with egg mixture. Bake 35 to 40 minutes or until wooden skewer inserted in center of bread comes out clean. Cool on wire rack.

16 servings.
Preparation time: 35 minutes.
Ready to serve: 4 hours, 50 minutes.

Per serving: 215 calories, 5 g fat (1.5 g saturated fat), 15 mg cholesterol, 200 mg sodium, 2.5 g fiber.

> **BAKER'S NOTE**
> • Dutch-process cocoa is less acidic, smoother and mellower in flavor than American-style cocoa. It also offers a richer, darker color.

VARIATION   Prune And Chocolate Bread

Substitute 1 cup chopped pitted dried plums (prunes) for the cherries (do not soak).

PRICOT ALMOND TEA TWIST

Swedish tea rings are beautiful examples of how simple preparations can be easily transformed into works of art.

DOUGH
- ½ recipe *Sweet Yeast Dough* (page 37)
- 2 tablespoons butter, softened
- ½ cup chopped toasted slivered almonds

FILLING
- 1 cup finely chopped dried apricots

- ¼ cup sugar
- ⅔ cup orange juice

ICING
- 1 recipe *Almond Glaze* (page 41) or powdered sugar

❶ Prepare dough as directed in recipe, using brown sugar. Cover large baking sheet with foil; grease. After first rising, punch dough down; turn out onto lightly floured surface. Roll dough into 15x10-inch rectangle.

❷ To make filling: In medium saucepan, combine dried apricots, sugar and orange juice. Bring mixture to a boil; reduce heat to medium-low. Cook, covered, 10 minutes or until thick, stirring occasionally. Cool.

❸ Spread dough with butter, then apricot filling to within ½ inch of edges. Sprinkle with almonds. Roll up jelly-roll fashion, beginning at long edge (see Baker's Note). Cut roll in half lengthwise. Place strips, filling sides up and side by side, on baking sheet. Twist together gently and loosely. Cover; let rise 30 minutes or until doubled in size.

❹ Heat oven to 350°F. Bake 25 to 30 minutes or until golden brown. Remove to wire rack; cool 10 minutes.

❺ Drizzle twists with glaze or dust with powdered sugar.

16 servings.

Preparation time: 30 minutes.

Ready to serve: 2 hours, 55 minutes.

Per serving: 205 calories, 5 g fat (2.5 g saturated fat), 25 mg cholesterol, 105 mg sodium, 1.5 g fiber.

BAKER'S NOTE
- As you twist this loaf, it's a bit sticky with the exposed fruit filling. Persevere, as the filling will hold to the dough and create a chewy topping on the coffee cake as it bakes. Cover the baking sheet with foil to eliminate pan scrubbing.

CHOCOLATE SOUR CREAM ZEBRA DOUGHNUTS

Regular or munchkin size, these are denser "cake" doughnuts, raised with baking powder. Yeasted doughnuts are lighter and airier, but these are still my favorite style. The 15 pounds I gained my college freshman year can be directly traced to late evening calls to a doughnut shop close to campus — trying to find out when the next batch of doughnuts was coming out of the fryer! These are dubbed zebra because they are comprised of dark chocolate dough, and dipped in a white chocolate glaze.

DOUGHNUTS

2	eggs
1⅓	cups sugar
1	cup dairy sour cream
2	teaspoons vanilla
2¾	cups unbleached all-purpose flour
⅓	cup unsweetened cocoa
2	teaspoons baking powder
1	teaspoon baking soda
½	teaspoon salt
½	teaspoon ground ginger
	Vegetable oil for frying

GLAZE

½	cup heavy cream
4	oz. white chocolate coarsely chopped
1	tablespoon butter
	Toasted shredded coconut

❶ In large bowl, combine eggs and sugar; beat well. Beat in sour cream and vanilla.

❷ In medium bowl, combine flour, cocoa, baking powder, baking soda, salt and ginger; blend well. Fold dry ingredients into egg mixture, blending until mixture forms very soft dough. Cover; refrigerate 30 to 60 minutes.

❸ Turn dough out onto lightly floured surface. Pat or roll dough to ½-inch thickness. With doughnut cutter or 3-inch round cutter, cut out 8 doughnuts. Use 1½-inch cutter to cut a hole in center of each 3-inch round. Refrigerate scraps of dough 15 minutes; pat out and cut more doughnuts. Place doughnuts and holes on parchment paper-lined baking sheets. Cover; refrigerate until ready to fry.

❹ Fill heavy Dutch oven or deep fryer with 3 inches of oil; heat to 375°F. Fry 3 doughnuts at a time. As soon as doughnuts float to the surface (about 1 minute), turn them and fry an additional 1 to 2 minutes or until golden brown. Fry doughnut holes, 6 at a time. Drain well on paper towels.

❺ To make glaze: Heat heavy cream in small saucepan over medium heat until just boiling. Remove from heat; stir in white chocolate and butter. Whisk until smooth. Cool until mixture starts to thicken slightly, stirring gently and occasionally (to avoid creating air bubbles).

❻ Place doughnuts and holes on wire rack. Drizzle with glaze; sprinkle with coconut. (Holes can be dipped in glaze and rolled in coconut.)

12 servings.

Preparation time: 30 minutes.

Ready to serve: 2 hours, 15 minutes.

Per serving: 450 calories, 24 g fat (9.5 g saturated fat), 65 mg cholesterol, 325 mg sodium, 1.5 g fiber.

DOUGHNUT FRYING TIPS

Here are tips, techniques and strategies on how to make doughnuts like an old pro.

- Use a light neutral oil, like canola (or a mixture of shortening and oil).
- Oil temperature is important — try to maintain at 375°F, otherwise doughnuts will burn or become heavy and greasy — use a heavy Dutch oven with a deep-frying thermometer, an electric skillet or a deep fryer.
- Only fry a few at a time, and allow oil temperature to stabilize between batches.
- Use a metal spatula dipped into hot oil to help transfer doughnuts to the oil — this helps maintain the doughnuts' shape.
- Remove from oil with a slotted spatula or spoon; drain well on paper towels. Serve while still warm or within a few hours of frying.
- Cut-out doughnuts can be refrigerated up to 6 hours before frying.
- To toast coconut, place in a dry skillet over medium heat. Cook, stirring occasionally, until light golden brown and slightly crisp. Or place on a baking sheet in a 350°F oven; bake 3 to 5 minutes or until golden and fragrant.

LEMON-FILLED DANISH PINWHEELS

Anise and lemon peel flavor the bread, while the pinwheel filling flavors can vary according to taste.

3 to 3½ cups unbleached all-purpose flour
1 (¼-oz.) pkg. active dry yeast
1 cup milk
⅓ cup sugar
3 tablespoons butter, cut up
2 teaspoons grated lemon peel

1 teaspoon each anise seeds, salt
¼ cup each whipped cream cheese, jarred lemon curd or peach, raspberry or blueberry preserves
1 egg beaten with 1 tablespoon water
Coarse or pearl sugar, if desired

❶ In large bowl, combine 1¼ cups of the flour and yeast. In medium saucepan or microwave-safe bowl, heat milk, ⅓ cup sugar, butter, lemon peel, anise seeds and salt until very warm (120°F to 130°F). Add to flour mixture; beat at low speed 30 seconds. Beat at high speed 3 minutes. By hand, stir in enough flour to create manageable dough.

❷ Turn dough out onto floured surface. Knead in enough remaining flour to create moderately soft dough that is smooth and elastic (3 to 5 minutes). Place dough in greased bowl; turn dough greased side up. Cover; let rise in warm place 1 hour or until doubled in size.

❸ Grease 2 large baking sheets. Punch dough down; turn out onto lightly floured board. Divide dough in half. Roll each half into 10x10-inch square. Cut into 5-inch squares; place on baking sheets. With sharp knife, cut diagonal line from each corner of squares to about ½ inch from center of each square. Place 1 teaspoon each of cream cheese and lemon curd in center of each square. Fold alternate points of dough over filling. Lightly but firmly press center of pastry to stick overlapping points together. Place on baking sheets. Repeat with other half of dough. Cover; let rise 45 minutes or until nearly doubled in size.

❹ Heat oven to 350°F. Brush pinwheels with egg mixture; sprinkle with coarse sugar. Bake 15 to 18 minutes or until golden brown. Cool on wire racks.

8 servings.
Preparation time: 40 minutes.
Ready to serve: 3 hours, 20 minutes.
Per serving: 310 calories, 7.5 g fat (4.5 g saturated fat), 40 mg cholesterol, 360 mg sodium, 1.5 g fiber.

HONEY PISTACHIO BEAR CLAWS

These favorite "Danishes" (small coffee cakes) are usually made with a Danish pastry dough that is layered with butter. The egg dough used here is just as delicious, but is easier to handle and takes less time to make.

½ recipe *Enriched Egg Dough* (page 30)
1 cup unsalted shelled pistachio nuts
½ cup sugar
2 tablespoons butter, softened
1 egg
1 egg beaten with 1 teaspoon water
1 recipe *Honey Glaze* (page 41)

❶ Prepare dough as directed. To make filling: Finely chop pistachios (by hand or in food processor). Mix with sugar, butter and egg; set aside.

❷ Grease 2 large baking sheets. After first rising, punch dough down. Turn dough out onto lightly floured surface; roll into 16x12-inch rectangle. Cut into 12 (4-inch) squares. Working with 1 square at a time, spread generous tablespoonful of filling across about 3 inches of square. Brush edges with egg mixture. Fold top of square over filling to form rectangle; press edges firmly to seal.

❸ With sharp knife, make ¾-inch cuts in dough about ½ inch apart along long sealed edge. Curve each roll slightly so the "claws" open up. Place on baking sheets. Cover; let rise in warm place 45 to 60 minutes.

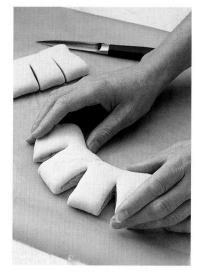

❹ Heat oven to 400°F. Brush dough with remaining egg mixture. Bake 12 minutes or until puffed and golden brown. Transfer to wire rack. Brush warm rolls with glaze.

12 servings.
Preparation time: 35 minutes.
Ready to serve: 3 hours, 15 minutes.
Per serving: 385 calories, 19 g fat (8.5 g saturated fat), 105 mg cholesterol, 100 mg sodium, 2 g fiber.

VARIATION Chocolate Streusel Bear Claws

Prepare dough as directed. Mix ½ cup sugar, ¼ cup unbleached all-purpose flour, 2 tablespoons butter, 1½ teaspoons unsweetened cocoa and ½ teaspoon ground cinnamon until crumbly. Sprinkle over 4-inch rolled dough squares. Continue as directed at Step 2.

MAPLE WALNUT FAN TAN LOAF

To serve this pull-apart bread, gently break into servings and spread with maple butter or drizzle with warm maple syrup.

DOUGH
- 1 (¼-oz.) pkg. active dry yeast
- ¼ cup warm water (105°F to 115°F)
- ¼ cup packed brown sugar
- ½ cup dairy sour cream
- ⅓ cup butter, melted
- 2 eggs
- 1 teaspoon salt
- 3 to 3½ cups unbleached all-purpose flour

FILLING
- 6 tablespoons butter, softened
- ½ cup granulated maple sugar
- ½ cup chopped black walnuts

❶ To make dough: In large bowl, dissolve yeast in water; let stand 5 minutes. Stir in brown sugar, sour cream, melted butter, eggs and salt. Gradually stir in enough of the flour to create manageable dough.

❷ Turn dough out onto lightly floured surface. Knead 5 minutes or until smooth and elastic (this will be soft dough). Place in greased bowl; turn dough greased side up. Cover; let rise in warm place 1 hour or until doubled in size.

❸ Grease 9x5-inch loaf pan. Punch dough down. Turn dough out onto lightly floured surface; roll into 20x12-inch rectangle. Spread dough with softened butter; sprinkle with maple sugar and walnuts. With sharp knife, cut rectangle crosswise into 5 (12x4-inch) strips. Stack 5 strips evenly on top of each other (the filling on top piece may fall off a bit — just press any nuts back on). Slice stack crosswise through all layers into 6 (4x2-inch) strips. Place layered strips, cut side up, side by side in bottom of pan. Cover; let rise 45 minutes or until doubled in size.

❹ Heat oven to 375°F. Bake 40 to 45 minutes or until golden brown, tenting loaf with foil for the last 15 minutes of baking. Cool 15 minutes. Remove from pan; cool on wire rack.

12 servings.
Preparation time: 40 minutes.
Ready to serve: 3 hours, 15 minutes.
Per serving: 325 calories, 17 g fat (8.5 g saturated fat), 70 mg cholesterol, 285 mg sodium, 1.5 g fiber.

SWEET BRUNCH BISCUITS WITH CHOCOLATE GRAVY

Sweet biscuit dough is closely related to scones and shortcakes. These biscuits are rich and decadent served for brunch, topped with fresh berries and doused with a smooth chocolate sauce.

BISCUITS

1	(8-oz.) container dairy sour cream
1	egg, beaten
1	cup packed dark brown sugar
½	teaspoon ground allspice or cloves
½	teaspoon ground cinnamon
2½ to 2¾	cups unbleached all-purpose flour
¾	teaspoon baking soda
⅛	teaspoon salt
	Assorted fresh berries

WARM CHOCOLATE GRAVY

½	cup unsweetened cocoa
⅓	cup sugar
⅓	cup packed brown sugar
3	tablespoons butter or margarine
½	cup heavy cream

❶ Heat oven to 375°F. Grease large baking sheet.

❷ In large bowl, combine sour cream, egg, 1 cup brown sugar, allspice and cinnamon. In medium bowl, stir together 2½ cups of the flour, baking soda and salt. Add flour mixture to sour cream mixture; stir just to combine. Turn dough out onto floured surface. Knead 10 to 12 strokes. Pat or lightly roll dough to ½-inch thickness; cut with floured 2½-inch round cutter. Place biscuits on baking sheet. Bake 12 to 15 minutes or until bottoms are browned. Remove from pan; cool slightly. Serve warm, split in half and topped with fresh berries.

❸ To make gravy: In small bowl, combine cocoa, sugar and ⅓ cup brown sugar. In small saucepan, melt butter over medium heat; stir in heavy cream. Bring nearly to a boil. Stir in cocoa mixture, whisking constantly 1 to 2 minutes or until sugar is dissolved and mixture is smooth and thickened. Drizzle over biscuits.

14 servings.

Preparation time: 30 minutes.

Ready to serve: 50 minutes.

Per serving: 275 calories, 9.5 g fat (5.5 g saturated fat), 40 mg cholesterol, 125 mg sodium, 2.5 g fiber.

BAKER'S NOTE

• You can also serve these biscuits with fruit and warm maple or berry syrup.

QUICK BREADS

The art of making great quick-rising breads (like biscuits, soda bread, muffins and cornbread) is to handle the dough or batter quickly and gently. In fact, the less you do to the dough or batter, the better the final outcome! Whip up the following breads just before mealtime to add zest and aroma to your table.

Dixie Biscuits, page 134

IRISH SODA BREAD

In Ireland the traditional breads evolved to suit both the ingredients and the cooking capabilities of the times. Because of the climate, only soft wheat could grow, so Irish breads developed from using soft wheat flour and the popular milk of the time, buttermilk. Soda bread is very versatile and appears in many forms — as a round cake, as individual rolls or scones, baked in the oven or on a griddle or even in a large covered pan over an open fire.

2½ cups unbleached all-purpose flour	2 tablespoons butter or margarine
2 cups stone-ground whole wheat flour	1 cup golden raisins
1 tablespoon sugar	1 tablespoon caraway seeds
2½ teaspoons baking soda	1 tablespoon grated orange peel
1 teaspoon salt	1½ cups buttermilk
	2 large eggs

❶ Heat oven to 400°F. Grease large baking sheet.

❷ In large bowl, combine 2 cups of the all-purpose flour, whole wheat flour, sugar, baking soda and salt; mix well. Cut butter into mixture with pastry blender or fork until well blended. Stir in raisins, caraway seeds and orange peel.

❸ Whisk buttermilk and eggs together. Stir into flour mixture, mixing with wooden spoon until dough forms a ball. Turn dough out onto floured surface, working in as much remaining ½ cup all-purpose flour as needed to make soft but not sticky dough. Knead lightly 1 minute, shaping dough into 8-inch round loaf. Place dough on baking sheet; flatten slightly. With floured knife slash a deep "X" across the top.

❹ Bake 40 to 45 minutes or until loaf sounds hollow when tapped on bottom. Remove from oven and serve warm, at room temperature or toasted.

18 servings.
Preparation time: 20 minutes.
Ready to serve: 1 hour, 15 minutes.
Per serving: 165 calories, 3 g total fat (1.5 g saturated fat), 30 mg cholesterol, 340 mg sodium 2.5 g fiber.

BAKER'S NOTES

- Buttermilk, the milk left after butter is churned, is also called sour milk. When added to flour along with bicarbonate of soda (called baking or bread soda), a chemical reaction occurs between the acidic buttermilk and alkaline soda that causes the gas production that leavens baked goods.

- A substitute for buttermilk is soured or "clabbered" milk: 1 cup buttermilk equals 1 teaspoon vinegar plus enough regular milk to make 1 cup. Stir and let stand until milk begins to curdle.

CREAM TEA SCONES

Afternoon tea, especially in England and Scotland, is never complete without at least a few currant scones and some other sweet cakes. Larger scones, filled with chocolate, nuts and dried fruits, have become popular with coffee in the U.S.

½ cup dried currants or raisins	¼ teaspoon salt
½ cup Madeira or Marsala wine	6 tablespoons butter or margarine
2½ to 3 cups unbleached all-purpose flour	1 cup half-and-half
¼ cup sugar	2 eggs
2 teaspoons baking powder	Granulated or coarse sugar, if desired

❶ In small bowl, combine currants and wine. Let stand 30 minutes; drain well.

❷ Heat oven to 375°F. In large bowl, combine 2½ cups of the flour, ¼ cup sugar, baking powder and salt; mix well. Cut butter into mixture with pastry blender until mixture resembles small crumbs; stir in drained currants. Whisk half-and-half and 1 of the eggs together. Stir into dry ingredients just until dough leaves side of bowl and forms soft dough.

❸ Turn dough out onto surface dusted with remaining ½ cup flour. Knead lightly, just enough to shape into a round. Roll or pat out dough to about ¾-inch thickness. Cut out scones with 2½- or 3-inch round cutter (or cut into any shape you like). Place on baking sheet. Beat remaining egg with 1 tablespoon water; brush over tops of scones; sprinkle with sugar. Bake 18 to 20 minutes or until golden brown. Cool on wire rack. Serve with raspberry jam and clotted or whipped cream.

12 servings.
Preparation time: 45 minutes.
Ready to serve: 1 hour, 10 minutes.
Per serving: 225 calories, 9 g total fat (5.5 g saturated fat), 60 mg cholesterol, 190 mg sodium 1 g fiber.

> **BAKER'S NOTES**
> • Toast oats in an ungreased baking pan in a 350°F oven 15 to 20 minutes or until light brown.
> • Dried currants are actually dried small Zante or Champagne grapes — they are not related to the red currant berries.

VARIATION Ginger Scones

Substitute ½ cup chopped crystallized ginger for the currants.

VARIATION Apricot White Chocolate Scones

Substitute 1 cup toasted oats for 1 cup of the flour. Stir ⅓ cup snipped dried apricots and ½ cup white chocolate chips into dry ingredients before adding milk and eggs. Pat dough into 9-inch round loaf on baking sheet. Cut into 8 wedges, but do not separate. Brush with egg and sprinkle with sugar or additional oats, if desired. Bake in a 375°F oven 25 to 30 minutes or until golden brown. Remove from baking sheet; carefully separate into wedges. Serve warm.

TOASTED FENNEL FIG SKILLET BREAD

Fennel seeds and dried figs seem so compatible — the flavors just seem to go together. Falling somewhat into the biscuit/scone camp, this easy bread is quickly cooked on the stove top.

1	teaspoon fennel seeds	¼	teaspoon baking soda
1⅓	cups unbleached all-purpose flour	2	tablespoons cold butter or margarine
⅔	cup rye flour		
1½	teaspoons baking powder	1	cup buttermilk
½	teaspoon salt	½	cup snipped dried figs

❶ In heavy, large 10-inch skillet over medium-low heat, toast fennel seeds 3 minutes or just until fragrant, shaking skillet frequently to prevent burning. Remove seeds from pan. Set skillet aside to cool.

❷ In large bowl, combine toasted fennel seeds, all-purpose flour, rye flour, baking powder, salt and baking soda. Cut butter into flour mixture with pastry blender or 2 knives until mixture resembles coarse crumbs. Using fork, stir in buttermilk and figs just until moistened.

❸ Turn dough out onto well-floured surface. Knead dough 10 to 12 strokes until nearly smooth. Roll or pat dough into circle about 7 inches in diameter and ¾-inch thick. Cut into 8 wedges with floured knife.

❹ Spray cooled skillet with nonstick cooking spray. Heat over medium-low heat 1 to 3 minutes or until drop of water sizzles on it. Carefully place dough wedges in skillet.

❺ Cover; cook 20 to 25 minutes or until golden brown and wooden pick inserted into side of a wedge comes out clean (turn wedges several times to brown both sides, spraying skillet with more nonstick spray if needed). Adjust heat level if necessary to prevent overbrowning. Serve bread warm.

8 servings.

Preparation time: 15 minutes.

Ready to serve: 45 minutes.

Per serving: 180 calories, 4 g total fat (2.5 g saturated fat), 10 mg cholesterol, 325 mg sodium 3 g fiber.

BAKER'S NOTE

• Dried figs should be sweet smelling and slightly moist. The two varieties most common in the U.S. are the light-colored Calimyrna and the dark purple Mission fig. Both kinds are grown in California. They are available in most grocery stores with other dried fruits, in the natural foods section or at co-op groceries in the bulk food area.

ILLED HAVARTI PAN BISCUITS

Havarti is a soft white cheese from Denmark. Its dill-flavored version always shines through, and here boosts the richness and taste of simple pan biscuits.

⅓	cup butter or margarine
2¼	cups unbleached all-purpose flour
1	cup (4 oz.) shredded dilled Havarti cheese
1	tablespoon baking powder
½	teaspoon salt
1	cup milk

❶ Heat oven to 400°F. Place butter in 9-inch square pan; melt in oven, about 4 minutes. Remove pan from oven.

❷ Meanwhile, in medium bowl, combine flour, cheese, baking powder and salt. Stir in milk just until soft dough forms.

❸ Turn dough out onto lightly floured surface. Knead 1 minute or until smooth. Pat or roll dough into 12x6-inch rectangle. Cut into 12 (1-inch) strips. Dip each strip into melted butter in pan. Fold strip in half. Place folded strips in 2 rows in same pan. Bake 20 to 25 minutes or until lightly browned.

12 servings.

Preparation time: 20 minutes.

Ready to serve: 45 minutes.

Per serving: 180 calories, 9 g total fat (5.5 g saturated fat), 25 mg cholesterol, 320 mg sodium 0.5 g fiber.

SETTLER'S CORNBREAD

Many favorite American breads feature cornmeal, from quick-leavened pan and skillet breads to fry breads and more involved yeast breads. Featured here is a rendition of a simple Western-style pan bread — it is dense, lightly sweet and tastes very much of corn.

1 egg	⅓ cup unbleached all-purpose or whole wheat flour
3 tablespoons sugar	
½ teaspoon salt	2 tablespoons olive oil or bacon fat
1 cup buttermilk	¼ cup chopped green onions, garlic chives or whole kernel corn.
1 teaspoon baking soda	
⅔ cup stone-ground yellow cornmeal	

❶ Heat oven to 375°F. Grease 8-inch square or round pan. In medium bowl, whisk egg, sugar and salt together. Whisk in buttermilk and baking soda. Beat in cornmeal, flour and oil until batter is smooth. Stir in onions.

❷ Pour batter into pan. Bake 20 to 25 minutes or until wooden pick inserted in center comes out clean. Serve warm with honey.

8 servings.
Preparation time: 15 minutes.
Ready to serve: 48 minutes.
Per serving: 135 calories, 5 g total fat (1 g saturated fat), 30 mg cholesterol, 340 mg sodium 1 g fiber.

VARIATION   New Mexican Blue Cornsticks

Heat two or three greased cast-iron cornstick pans in 375°F oven 15 minutes. Substitute blue cornmeal for yellow cornmeal in batter. Reduce sugar to 1 tablespoon and add ½ teaspoon ground cumin and ½ teaspoon minced garlic. Stir in ¼ cup toasted coarsely chopped pine nuts. Pour batter into hot cornstick pans. Bake 20 minutes. Makes about 12 cornsticks.

BAKER'S NOTES

- This cornbread batter is thin because of the high proportion of buttermilk to cornmeal and flour. The bread doesn't rise high, but is very moist.
- If you want a crusty cornbread, using a preheated cast-iron skillet or cornstick pans will do the trick. Grease pan(s) with vegetable oil, then place in oven while it heats. Carefully take pan(s) out of oven to pour in batter; bake as directed. Regular baking pans are too thin to be preheated; only do this with heavy or enameled cast-iron pans.
- In New Mexico, blue cornmeal is common, creating baked goods that are greyish-blue in color but still have the same flavor as yellow cornmeal. Blue cornmeal is available in natural food stores and co-op groceries.

DIXIE BISCUITS

In the southern United States, where biscuit making is an art, buttermilk biscuits are the preferred formula — they are light, fluffy and slightly sour in flavor.

    2   cups unbleached all-purpose flour
    2   teaspoons baking powder
    ½   teaspoon each baking soda, salt
    ⅓   cup butter, lard or shortening
    ¾   to 1 cup buttermilk

❶ Heat oven to 425°F. In medium bowl, combine flour, baking powder, baking soda and salt; mix well. Cut in butter with pastry blender or fork until mixture resembles crumbs. Stir in enough buttermilk to form soft dough.

❷ Turn dough out onto lightly floured surface. Gently knead 8 to 10 times. Pat dough out to ½-inch thickness. Cut out biscuits with 2½- to 3-inch cutter or cut into 2-inch squares. Re-roll scraps and cut out more biscuits. Place biscuits on baking sheet or in ungreased 9-inch pan (biscuits on baking sheet will be darker and crisper, biscuits in pan will be lighter and fluffier). Bake 15 minutes or until golden brown. Serve hot.

About 8 servings.
Preparation time: 15 minutes.
Ready to serve: 30 minutes.
Per serving: 190 calories, 8.5 g total fat (5 g saturated fat), 25 mg cholesterol, 415 mg sodium 1 g fiber.

VARIATION   Sesame Biscuits

Stir in 2 teaspoons sesame seeds.

VARIATION   Cornmeal Biscuits

Use 1½ cups all-purpose flour and ½ cup yellow cornmeal.

VARIATION   Herb Biscuits

Stir in ½ teaspoon crumbled dried sage, ½ teaspoon celery seeds and ¼ teaspoon dried mustard.

BAKER'S NOTES
- When stamping out biscuits, cut straight down and pull the cutter straight back up to ensure an even rise during baking.
- If you do not have 2½- or 3-inch round cutters use the edge of a water glass, or just cut dough into squares or diamonds with a knife. Kids love making other shapes with cookie cutters too.

Tea breads can be made large or small. They're always welcomed as gifts, sell well at bake sales, and are the first thing to disappear on a tray of sweets at tea parties or other gatherings.

SOUTH PACIFIC BANANA BREAD

1 cup packed brown sugar	1 teaspoon baking soda
½ cup each vegetable oil, buttermilk	½ teaspoon salt
2 cups mashed very ripe bananas (about 5 medium)	½ cup each chopped macadamia nuts, toasted flaked coconut
2 eggs	⅓ cup chopped dried papaya, mango, apricots or pitted dates
1 teaspoon each vanilla, rum extract	
2½ cups unbleached all-purpose flour (or blend of half all-purpose and half whole wheat flour)	

❶ Heat oven to 350°F. Grease 2 (8x4-inch) loaf pans. In large bowl, whisk sugar and oil together until well combined. Stir in buttermilk, bananas, eggs, vanilla and rum extract.

❷ Combine flour, baking soda and salt; stir into wet ingredients just until moistened. Stir in nuts, coconut and papaya. Pour batter evenly into prepared pans. Bake 55 to 60 minutes or until wooden pick inserted in center comes out clean. Cool 10 minutes; remove from pans. Cool completely on wire rack.

20 servings.
Preparation time: 25 minutes.
Ready to serve: 2 hours, 20 minutes.

Per serving: 215 calories, 9 g total fat (2 g saturated fat), 20 mg cholesterol, 145 mg sodium 1.5 g fiber.

AZTEC CHOCOLATE LOAVES

3 oz. (3 squares) bittersweet baking chocolate, finely chopped	½ teaspoon ground allspice
½ cup butter or margarine	2 eggs, slightly beaten
3 cups unbleached all-purpose flour	1¼ cups milk
¾ cup sugar	2 teaspoons Mexican vanilla
1 teaspoon baking powder	2 (3-oz.) tablets Mexican chocolate, coarsely chopped
1 teaspoon ground cinnamon	1 recipe *Almond Glaze* (page 41)
1 teaspoon salt	Toasted sliced almonds
½ teaspoon baking soda	

❶ Heat oven to 350°F. Grease 2 (8x4-inch) loaf pans. In small saucepan or microwave, gently melt bittersweet chocolate and butter together just until smooth; cool.

❷ In large bowl, combine flour, sugar, baking powder, cinnamon, salt, baking soda and allspice. Stir in melted chocolate, eggs, milk and vanilla just until batter is moistened. Fold in Mexican chocolate. Spread batter into pans. Bake 40 to 45 minutes or until wooden pick inserted in center comes out clean. Cool 10 minutes; remove from pans. Cool completely on wire rack. Drizzle with glaze; sprinkle with almonds.

20 servings.
Preparation time: 30 minutes.
Ready to serve: 2 hours, 20 minutes.
Per serving: 245 calories, 10.5 g total fat (6 g saturated fat), 35 mg cholesterol, 220 mg sodium 1.5 g fiber.

SUGARED ROSEMARY-LEMON LOAF

½ cup golden raisins
1 cup milk
1 tablespoon minced fresh rosemary
2 eggs
¼ cup light olive oil
¾ cup plus 2 tablespoons sugar

2 cups unbleached all-purpose flour
2 teaspoons baking powder
1 tablespoon plus 2 teaspoons grated lemon peel
¼ teaspoon salt

❶ Heat oven to 350°F. Grease 9x5-inch loaf pan.

❷ In small saucepan, combine raisins, milk and rosemary over medium heat. Simmer gently 2 minutes; cool.

❸ In medium bowl, whisk eggs, oil and ¾ cup of the sugar. Combine flour, baking powder, 1 tablespoon of the lemon peel and salt. Stir into egg mixture; mix until batter is smooth. Stir in milk mixture; beat until smooth. Combine remaining 2 tablespoons sugar and 2 teaspoons grated lemon peel. Pour batter into pan; sprinkle evenly with lemon-sugar mixture. Bake 45 to 48 minutes or until wooden pick inserted in center comes out clean. Cool 10 minutes; turn out onto wire rack to cool completely.

12 servings.
Preparation time: 20 minutes.
Ready to serve: 2 hours, 10 minutes.
Per serving: 215 calories, 6 g total fat (1 g saturated fat), 35 mg cholesterol, 150 mg sodium 1 g fiber.

BAKER'S NOTES

• Grease the entire inside of loaf pans or spray with nonstick cooking spray.

• Use a wooden pick inserted in center of quick bread loaves to test for doneness — the pick should come out clean. The tops of the loaves should also be firm to the touch in the center and be pulling away from sides of the pan.

• Run the tip of a knife around the edges of the pan to be sure the loaves release easily when you tip them out of the pan.

ZUCCHINI CHOCOLATE CHUNK MUFFINS WITH PISTACHIO STREUSEL

These moist, sweet gems taste like individual coffee cakes. For variation, make these larger in a Texas-style muffin pan or as small tea breads in a mini muffin tin.

STREUSEL

⅓ cup coarsely chopped shelled pistachios

2 tablespoons packed brown sugar

2 tablespoons unbleached all-purpose flour

¼ teaspoon ground cinnamon

1 tablespoon butter or margarine, softened

MUFFINS

2 cups unbleached all-purpose flour

½ cup sugar

1 tablespoon baking powder

1 teaspoon ground cinnamon

¼ teaspoon salt

1 cup milk

¼ cup vegetable oil

2 eggs

1 teaspoon vanilla

1 cup shredded zucchini

½ cup chopped semisweet chocolate or baking chips

❶ Heat oven to 400°F. Grease bottoms only of 12 muffin cups. To make streusel: In small bowl, combine pistachios, brown sugar, 2 tablespoons flour and ¼ teaspoon cinnamon. Cut butter into dry ingredients with fork until crumbly. Set aside.

❷ To make muffins: In large bowl, combine 2 cups flour, sugar, baking powder, 1 teaspoon cinnamon and salt; mix well. Whisk milk, oil, eggs and vanilla together. Stir into dry ingredients with zucchini, mixing just until all ingredients are moistened. Fold in chocolate. Spoon batter evenly into muffin cups; sprinkle with streusel. Bake 20 to 25 minutes or until golden brown. Remove muffins from cups; cool on wire rack.

12 servings.

Preparation time: 30 minutes.

Ready to serve: 1 hour, 30 minutes.

Per serving: 250 calories, 11 g total fat (3.5 g saturated fat), 40 mg cholesterol, 200 mg sodium 1.5 g fiber.

VARIATION   Fresh Raspberry Apple Muffins with Hazelnut Streusel

Substitute 1 cup fresh raspberries and ½ cup finely chopped fresh apple for the zucchini and chocolate. Stir in 1 tablespoon grated orange peel. Substitute chopped hazelnuts for the pistachios in streusel, if desired.

BAKER'S NOTE

• Muffin cups are only greased on the bottom, so the batter will rise evenly, clinging to sides of cups.

FRESH RASPBERRY APPLE MUFFINS WITH HAZELNUT STREUSEL

STEAMED BOSTON BROWN BREAD

This is a classic example of a steamed bread, cooked in coffee cans to make upright loaves. Dense with whole grains and dried fruit, its spicy goodness is wonderful when thinly sliced and toasted, then slathered with butter. It's best served with Boston baked beans.

2	cups rye flour
2	cups whole wheat flour
2	cups stone-ground white or yellow cornmeal
2	teaspoons baking soda
1½	teaspoons salt
1	teaspoon ground allspice
1	quart buttermilk or sour milk
¾	cup molasses
1	cup chopped dried dates, dried cranberries, raisins or currants

❶ Grease 3 (11.5- to 13-oz.) empty clean coffee cans. In large bowl, combine rye flour, whole wheat flour, cornmeal, baking soda, salt and allspice. Whisk buttermilk and molasses together; stir into dry ingredients just until moistened. Fold in dates.

❷ Fill cans ⅔ full of batter. Cover each can tightly with aluminum foil, securing tops with rubber bands or kitchen twine. Place cans on rack in deep Dutch oven, canning kettle or steamer. Pour boiling water into pan halfway up sides of cans. Cover pan and steam 2 hours or until bamboo skewer inserted in center of breads comes out clean. Replenish water as necessary to maintain original level.

❸ Remove cans to wire rack; cool 10 minutes. Run thin metal spatula around edges of breads to loosen; slide loaves out. Serve warm or at room temperature, spread with butter or cream cheese.

24 servings.
Preparation time: 20 minutes.
Ready to serve: 3 hours, 20 minutes.

Per serving: 170 calories, 1.5 g total fat (0.5 g saturated fat), 5 mg cholesterol, 290 mg sodium 3.5 g fiber.

VARIATION   Blueberry Ginger Brown Bread

Substitute honey for the molasses and dried or fresh wild blueberries for the dates. Stir in 3 tablespoons grated fresh ginger.

BAKER'S NOTES

• You may need to use 2 pans to steam all loaves at the same time, unless you have a large canning kettle.

• If you prefer, you can bake the loaves in cans in a 300°F oven 1½ hours or until a bamboo skewer inserted in the center comes out clean.

NATIVE AMERICAN FRY BREAD

Fry bread is one of the most widespread of Native American foods. It's part of everyday cooking, as well as celebration times. The recipe varies from region to tribe, but basically flour, baking powder, salt and water or milk are the main ingredients.

2½   cups unbleached all-purpose flour
2   teaspoons baking powder
1   teaspoon salt
1   tablespoon vegetable oil, lard or shortening
1   cup warm milk or water
       Vegetable oil, shortening or lard for deep frying
1   recipe *Indian Spiced Honey* (page 38) or powdered sugar

❶ In medium bowl, combine flour, baking powder and salt; mix well. With fork, work 1 tablespoon oil into dry mixture until crumbly.

❷ Stir in milk with fork just until dough holds together. Turn dough out onto floured surface; knead gently 3 minutes. Cover; let rest 15 minutes. Begin heating oil for frying.

❸ Divide dough into 8 balls. Pat or roll dough into rounds 6 to 7 inches in diameter. Slide dough rounds, 1 at a time, into hot oil (about 380°F). Dough will puff immediately; cook it on one side 1 minute, then turn over to finish browning. Remove from oil; drain well on paper towels. Continue with remaining dough, being careful that oil stays hot enough. Serve warm with honey or dusted with powdered sugar.

8 servings.
Preparation time: 35 minutes.
Ready to serve: 55 minutes.
Per serving: 320 calories, 12 g total fat (2 g saturated fat), 0 mg cholesterol, 430 mg sodium 1 g fiber.

VARIATION   Fry Bread with Spiced Syrup
Bring 2 cups water, ¾ cup packed dark brown sugar, 1½ teaspoons anise seeds, 3 whole allspice and 1 small cinnamon stick to a boil. Simmer, uncovered, until thick and syrupy. Cool; strain spices. Serve warm with bread.

FLAT BREADS

When a risen yeast dough is rolled or patted very thin before rising, it produces loaves of flatbread, usually no more than ½-inch high, with thick crusts and chewy interiors. These breads bake quickly and are extremely versatile. Flatbreads can be appetite teasers, or meals in themselves. Some flatbreads, like cracker bread or chapati, are unleavened tender doughs — as quick to prepare and bake as to enjoy.

Arabian Pita Pockets, page 155

PIZZA DOUGH

Making your own crust dough for homemade pizza is so far and away better than take-out or frozen. But be forewarned: It will be hard to go back!

1	cup water	1½	cups whole wheat flour	
2	tablespoons olive oil	1½	cups unbleached all-purpose flour	
2	teaspoons honey	1	tablespoon yeast	
1½	teaspoons minced garlic		Cornmeal	
1	teaspoon salt			

❶ Place water, oil, honey, garlic, salt, whole wheat flour, all-purpose flour and yeast in 1½-lb. loaf bread machine, following manufacturer's instructions. Select Dough cycle; press Start.

❷ Remove dough from machine when cycle is finished; let rest 10 minutes.

❸ Heat oven to 450°F, with baking stone on bottom oven rack, if desired. Sprinkle cornmeal on large baking sheet or pizza paddle (peel). Divide dough in half. Form each piece of dough into 10- to 12-inch round; place on baking sheet or paddle. Add toppings of choice. Slide pizzas onto baking stone in oven* or put baking sheets in oven. Bake 12 to 15 minutes or until golden brown and crust is cooked through in center (test with wooden pick or tip of knife). Serve hot.

TIP *If you have only one oven, roll out second half of dough and top while first one is baking.

Dough for 12 servings.
Preparation time: 15 minutes.
Ready to serve: 2 hours, 10 minutes.
Per serving: 135 calories, 2.5 g total fat (0.5 g saturated fat), 0 mg cholesterol, 195 mg sodium, 2.5 g fiber.

PIZZA TOPPINGS

Here are a few out-of-the ordinary suggestions for pizza toppings that will take your pizzas beyond pepperoni. Be sure to use a light hand when topping dough, so it can rise and bake properly; an overloaded pizza will stay doughy in the center and have overbaked edges.

- Red onion wedges, fresh thyme and shredded Gruyère cheese.
- Artichoke hearts and smoked Provolone.
- Roasted red bell pepper strips, basil pesto and shredded Romano cheese.
- Sliced plum tomato, fresh basil and smoked or fresh mozzarella.
- Sautéed spinach, bay shrimp, feta cheese and kalamata olives.
- Sautéed wild mushrooms (porcini, shiitake, crimini, etc.).

ROASTED GARLIC-FENNEL FLATBREADS

You'll need to plan ahead for these individual flatbreads, roasting pungent garlic and fragrant fennel to bring out their natural sweetness and allowing them to cool so they can become a part of — and topping for — the dough.

1 large head garlic, top ¼ of bulb sliced off	2½ to 3 cups unbleached bread flour
2 medium fennel bulbs, trimmed, halved, thinly sliced (about 1½ lb. trimmed)	1 cup semolina flour
	1 tablespoon grated orange peel
	1½ teaspoons salt
2 tablespoons olive oil, plus additional for brushing flatbreads	½ teaspoon freshly ground pepper
	Cornmeal or semolina flour
1 (¼-oz.) pkg. active dry yeast	Kosher (coarse) salt, if desired
1 cup warm water (105°F to 115°F)	

❶ Heat oven to 375°F. Place garlic head and fennel in foil-lined 13x9-inch pan. Drizzle with 2 tablespoons oil. Cover tightly with foil; bake 45 minutes or until vegetables are golden brown. Cool; squeeze garlic from paper skins. (This may be done ahead; cover and refrigerate separately until ready to use.)

❷ In large bowl, dissolve yeast in water; let stand 5 minutes. Stir in 2½ cups of the bread flour, semolina, garlic paste, orange peel, salt and pepper; mix until soft dough forms. Turn out onto surface dusted with remaining ½ cup flour. Knead 6 to 8 minutes or until dough is smooth and elastic. Place dough in greased bowl; turn greased side up and let rise 1 hour or until doubled in size.

❸ Sprinkle cornmeal on 2 large baking sheets. Punch dough down. Turn out onto floured surface; divide into 4 equal pieces. Flatten each piece into rounds about ½-inch thick. Place 2 dough rounds on each baking sheet. Prick dough all over with fork. Brush with olive oil, and evenly distribute roasted fennel on top of each round. Sprinkle with salt. Let rest while oven is heating.

❹ Heat oven to 450°F, with baking stone on lowest oven rack, if desired. Spray inside of oven with water, then quickly slide 2 rounds of dough onto baking stone or bake all 4 on baking sheets. Bake 12 to 15 minutes or until golden and crisp. Remove from oven and repeat with remaining rounds, if necessary.

16 servings.
Preparation time: 1 hour.
Ready to serve: 18 hours.
Per serving: 150 calories, 3 g total fat (0.5 g saturated fat), 0 mg cholesterol, 235 mg sodium, 2 g fiber.

CRISP CRACKER BREADS

These are made from an unyeasted wheat dough — thin, crispy, irregularly shaped rounds that can be topped with whatever strikes your fancy or taste.

CRACKERS

2	cups whole wheat flour
1	cup unbleached all-purpose flour
1	teaspoon salt
¼	teaspoon cayenne pepper
2	tablespoons olive oil
1	cup warm water
1	egg white beaten with 1 tablespoon water

TOPPINGS

Kosher (coarse) salt

Sesame seeds

Anise seeds

Cumin seeds

Hulled pumpkin seeds, coarsely chopped

Unsalted sunflower seeds

❶ Place whole wheat flour, all-purpose flour, 1 teaspoon salt and cayenne in food processor. With motor running, add oil and water in steady stream. Process 10 seconds or until ball of dough forms. If dough is too sticky, add a few tablespoons flour. If dough is dry, add a few tablespoons water (you want soft dough).

❷ Process dough about 1 minute longer. Turn dough out onto lightly floured surface. Knead 30 seconds or until smooth and elastic. Transfer to greased bowl; turn dough greased side up. Cover; let rest 1 hour.

❸ Heat oven to 425°F. Grease 2 large baking sheets. Divide dough into 4 equal pieces. Roll each piece into 10-inch round, about ¹⁄₁₆-inch thick. Transfer to baking sheets. Brush with egg white mixture; sprinkle with desired seed toppings. Bake 12 minutes or until lightly puffed and golden brown.

16 servings.

Preparation time: 20 minutes.

Ready to serve: 1 hours, 30 minutes.

Per serving: 95 calories, 2 g total fat (0.5 g saturated fat), 0 mg cholesterol, 150 mg sodium, 2 g fiber.

BAKER'S NOTE

• Use any combination of suggested toppings in combination, or just one kind per cracker. The amount you use is up to your personal taste.

MILANESE FOCACCIA

A thick, chewy flatbread, this Italian country hearth bread comes covered with a seemingly endless array of roasted vegetable toppings, from eggplant and bell peppers to sun-dried tomatoes, thinly sliced potatoes and olives.

2¼ to 2½ cups unbleached all-purpose flour
   1 (¼-oz.) pkg. active dry yeast
   2½ teaspoons dried rosemary, crushed
   1 teaspoon salt
   1¼ cups very warm water (120°F to 130°F)
   2 tablespoons olive oil, plus additional for brushing dough
   ½ cup semolina flour, plus additional for dusting baking sheet
    Kosher (coarse) salt

❶ In large bowl, combine 1½ cups of the all-purpose flour, yeast, 1½ teaspoons of the rosemary and salt. Stir in water and 2 tablespoons oil. Beat with electric mixer 30 seconds at low speed; beat at high speed 3 minutes. By hand, stir in ½ cup semolina and enough all-purpose flour to create manageable dough (it will be soft). Turn dough out onto floured surface. Knead in enough remaining all-purpose flour to make medium-soft dough, 3 to 5 minutes or until smooth and elastic. Place in greased bowl; turn dough greased side up. Cover; let rise in warm place 45 to 60 minutes or until doubled in size.

❷ Punch dough down. Spray inside of jumbo resealable plastic bag with nonstick spray. Place dough inside; close bag, allowing room for dough to expand (Or keep dough in large bowl). Refrigerate 16 to 24 hours.

❸ Dust large baking sheet with semolina. Remove dough from bag. Place dough on baking sheet. Gently pull and stretch dough into 15x8-inch rectangle. Cover loosely with clean kitchen towel; let rise in warm place 45 minutes or until nearly doubled in size.

❹ Heat oven to 450°F. Using the tips of your fingers, press deep indentations into surface of dough every 1½ to 2 inches. Cover again; let rest 10 minutes. Brush surface of dough lightly olive oil; sprinkle with remaining 1 teaspoon rosemary and kosher salt. Bake 16 to 18 minutes or until golden brown. Serve warm, cut into wedges or squares.

12 servings.
Preparation time: 30 minutes.
Ready to serve: 26 hours, 30 minutes.
Per serving: 135 calories, 3.5 g total fat (0.5 g saturated fat), 0 mg cholesterol, 325 mg sodium, 1 g fiber.

NEPALESE CHAPATI

Chapati are a softer cousin to the tortilla. They're traditionally baked on a cast-iron griddle (tava), skillet or in a tandoori oven, but can also be baked in a conventional Western-style oven. This is a non-yeasted dough, and the baked result is wonderful with vegetarian meals of lentils or vegetable stews.

1½ cups whole wheat flour
1 cup unbleached bread or all-purpose flour
1 teaspoon salt
½ cup warm water
2 tablespoons ghee or softened butter, if desired

❶ In large bowl, combine whole wheat flour, ½ cup of the all-purpose flour and salt. Make a well in center of flour mixture; gradually add water, mixing well to form soft dough. Turn dough out onto floured surface. Knead dough 8 to 10 minutes or until smooth and elastic. Cover; let rest 30 minutes or up to 2 hours.

❷ Divide dough into 12 equal pieces; roll each piece into a ball. Flatten each ball and dip in remaining ½ cup flour. Roll each flattened ball into 6-inch round flatbread.

❸ Heat cast-iron griddle or skillet over medium-high heat. When griddle is hot, place 1 chapati round on griddle. Cook 10 seconds or until it begins to brown and becomes firm enough to pick up; turn over. Cook additional 10 to 20 seconds or until light brown. Turn back over to first side. With folded clean kitchen towel or paper towel, gently but firmly press down on chapati, causing air bubble in the bread to expand.

❹ Remove chapati from griddle. Brush one side with ghee or butter. Wrap in clean kitchen towel to keep warm and soft. Repeat with remaining chapati.

12 servings.
Preparation time: 30 minutes.
Ready to serve: 1 hour, 12 minutes.

Per serving: 110 calories, 2.5 g total fat (1.5 g saturated fat), 5 mg cholesterol, 195 mg sodium, 2 g fiber.

BAKER'S NOTE
• Ghee is clarified butter that can be purchased in jars at Indian markets or made by melting butter over low heat. Gently simmer 15 to 25 minutes or until the milk solids settle to the bottom of the saucepan and turn light brown. Cool and strain through a cheesecloth. This clear golden butter keeps at room temperature in an airtight container for several weeks.

$\mathcal{T}$URKISH QUILTED PEDA BREAD

Another flatbread (called ekmek) *from the Armenian bakers of the Middle East, this loaf is also related to Italian focaccia. A staple country bread in Turkey, the oval shape with a ridged or quilted-looking top is the most common form. Other popular shapes include braids or rings, egg-washed and coated with sesame or poppy seeds.*

1	(¼-oz.) pkg. active dry yeast
1	tablespoon honey
1	cup warm water (105°F to 115°F)
1⅓	cups whole wheat flour
1¼ to 1¾	cups unbleached all-purpose flour
1	teaspoon salt
2	tablespoons olive oil or melted butter
1	egg beaten with 2 teaspoons water
2	tablespoons sesame seeds

❶ In large bowl, dissolve yeast and honey in water. Stir in whole wheat flour to form soft dough. Cover bowl; let sponge rest 30 minutes or until bubbly and risen.

❷ Stir in 1¼ cups of the all-purpose flour, salt and oil until firm dough forms.

❸ Turn dough out onto lightly floured surface. Knead about 10 minutes or until smooth and elastic. Put into greased bowl; turn dough greased side up. Cover; let rise in warm place 1½ to 2 hours or until doubled in size. Punch down; let rest 10 minutes.

❹ On lightly floured surface, flatten dough into oval round, 11x14 inches. Place on floured baking sheet. Cover; let rise 45 minutes or until doubled in size.

❺ Heat oven to 425°F. Using wet fingertips, push through dough to pan 1 inch from edge all around oval. Within oval, using blunt edge of knife, make 4 parallel indentations across dough, then 4 more indentations in the opposite direction to make criss-cross or quilted pattern (leave 1-inch border around edge). Brush dough with egg mixture; sprinkle with sesame seeds.

❻ Bake 20 to 25 minutes or until golden brown.

12 servings.
Preparation time: 35 minutes.
Ready to serve: 4 hours, 5 minutes.
Per serving: 130 calories, 3.5 g total fat (0.5 g saturated fat), 15 mg cholesterol, 200 mg sodium, 2.5 g fiber.

$\mathcal{P}$ROVENCAL FOUGASSE

Fougasse, part of a country hearth baking tradition in southern France, is one of several regional flatbreads. The word fougasse *(like focaccia, in Italy) has its root in the Latin word for hearth or fireplace.*

1	teaspoon active dry yeast
¾	cup warm water (105°F to 115°F)
1½ to 2	cups unbleached all-purpose flour
1	tablespoon olive oil, plus additional for brushing loaves
1	teaspoon salt
¾	cup whole wheat flour
1/3	cup buckwheat flour
	Herbes de Provence to taste, crushed

❶ In large bowl, dissolve yeast in water. Stir in 1 cup of the all-purpose flour; stir vigorously 1 minute. Cover bowl; let rest 30 minutes.

❷ Stir 1 tablespoon oil, salt, whole wheat flour and buckwheat flour into sponge. Add enough remaining all-purpose flour to make soft dough. Turn dough out onto lightly floured surface. Knead 5 minutes or until smooth and elastic. Place dough in greased bowl; turn dough greased side up. Cover; let rise in warm place 2 hours or until nearly doubled in size. Grease 2 large baking sheets. Punch dough down; divide into 2 equal pieces. Shape each piece into a ball; let rest 5 minutes. Working with 1 ball at a time, flatten with palms of hands into rectangle or oval, about 12x8 inches and about ½-inch thick. Transfer to baking sheets.

❸ Using sharp knife or razor blade, make 6 diagonal slits to resemble veins of a leaf or fat-runged ladder, cutting all the way through dough. Gently pull slits open so the bread keeps its lacy look. Cover; let rise 20 to 30 minutes or until puffy.

❹ Heat oven to 400°F. Brush loaves with oil; sprinkle with herbs. Bake 20 minutes or until golden brown. Serve warm.

12 servings.
Preparation time: 30 minutes.
Ready to serve: 3 hours.
Per serving: 110 calories, 2.5 g total fat (0.5 g saturated fat), 0 mg cholesterol, 195 mg sodium, 2 g fiber.

VARIATION   Starter Fougasse
For smaller appetizer loaves that can be shared, divide dough into 4 equal pieces. Flatten them into 6x4-inch ovals. Slash and let rise as directed. Bake 11 to 13 minutes or until golden brown.

ARABIAN PITA POCKETS

This style of puffed flatbread is known throughout the Middle East and Indian subcontinent, where it's baked in tandoori ovens, on flat griddles or in the oven. Open pita and fill with salads, meats or cheeses, or just serve warm as part of a meal.

1	(¼-oz.) pkg. active dry yeast
1½	cups warm water (105°F to 115°F)
1	teaspoon salt
3	tablespoons olive oil
2	cups whole wheat flour
2 to 2½	cups unbleached all-purpose flour
	Yellow cornmeal

❶ In large bowl, dissolve yeast in water. Stir in salt, oil and whole wheat flour; beat until smooth. Beat in as much of the all-purpose flour as needed to make firm dough (about 1¾ cups).

❷ Turn dough out onto lightly floured surface. Knead 10 minutes or until very smooth and elastic, adding remaining flour as needed to prevent sticking. Place in greased bowl; turn dough greased side up. Cover; let rise in warm place 1 to 1½ hours or until doubled in size.

❸ Heat oven to 450°F; have oven rack at lowest position. Sprinkle large baking sheets with cornmeal (or use baking stone with cornmeal or foil pieces directly on rack). Punch dough down; divide into 8 equal pieces. On lightly floured surface, roll or pat each piece into 7- to 8-inch round, ⅛-inch thick. Place on baking sheets. Bake on lowest rack 5 to 6 minutes or until puffed and lightly browned. Cool on wire rack 2 minutes covered with damp kitchen towel. Slip pitas, while still warm, into heavy plastic storage bags to soften.

8 servings.
Preparation time: 35 minutes.
Ready to serve: 2 hours, 5 minutes.
Per serving: 270 calories, 6 g total fat (1 g saturated fat), 0 mg cholesterol, 295 mg sodium, 5 g fiber.

VARIATION Appetizer Pitas
Divide dough into 16 pieces. Roll into 5-inch rounds, ⅛-inch thick. Bake as directed.

BAKER'S NOTE
• The magic of pocket bread is in the puffing caused by steam created inside the dough. To achieve this, a very hot oven is needed.

CELEBRATION BREADS

Special occasions, important gatherings and spiritual celebrations have always defined traditional cooking and baking. Certain breads and baked goods have become symbolic of times of thanksgiving, the eternal rhythm of the seasons, and happy times with those we love. Consider adding one of these enduring favorites to your repertoire.

Aromatic Seeded Challah, page 167

THANKSGIVING TURKEY TWIST

Here's a whimsical coffee cake to bake up for that Thanksgiving breakfast that is supposed to hold everyone until dinner!

DOUGH

½ cup packed brown sugar or granulated maple sugar

1½ teaspoons ground cinnamon

½ teaspoon each freshly ground nutmeg, ground allspice or freshly ground pepper

½ recipe *Sweet Yeast Dough* (page 37)

½ cup butter or margarine, softened

¾ cup snipped dried mixed fruit

Whole cloves or currants

1 egg, beaten

APPLE CIDER ICING

1 cup powdered sugar

1 to 3 tablespoons apple cider

⅛ teaspoon ground cinnamon

❶ In small bowl, stir together brown sugar, 1½ teaspoons cinnamon, nutmeg and allspice; set aside.

❷ Prepare dough as directed. Grease large baking sheet. After first rise, punch dough down. Turn dough out onto lightly floured surface. Roll dough into 20x12-inch rectangle. Spread dough with butter; sprinkle with spice-sugar mixture and dried fruit. Roll up jelly-roll fashion from long side; seal seam well. Trim about 1 inch from ends of roll; reserve trimmings. Seal ends; lay roll on baking sheet. Curve roll into loose "S" shape; decorate as photographed. Cover; let rise 45 minutes or until doubled in size.

❸ Heat oven to 350°F. Brush dough with egg. Bake 25 to 30 minutes or until golden brown. Remove from pan; cool on wire rack.

❹ Meanwhile, prepare icing: In medium bowl, mix powdered sugar, apple cider and ⅛ teaspoon cinnamon until smooth. Drizzle icing over sliced coffee cake.

12 servings.

Preparation time: 45 minutes.

Ready to serve: 4 hours, 10 minutes.

Per serving: 295 calories, 7.5 g total fat (4.5 g saturated fat), 50 mg cholesterol, 160 mg sodium, 2 g fiber.

BAKER'S NOTES

• Black peppercorns have a spicy sweetness that blend effortlessly with other spices. Try using either allspice or pepper in this bread; either one gives a burst of sweet heat.

• Use trimmed dough to create a wattle and feet for your turkey. Make feathers along its side with the edge of a pastry tip or a small round cookie cutter by pressing half-moon shapes in rows (see photo). Use a whole clove or dried currant for the eye.

CRIMSON CRANBERRY WREATHS

Sweet tart cranberries (or "crane" berries, named after the whooping cranes that savor them) are an eternal favorite during the fall baking and holiday season. A cranberry sauce enhanced by late summer raspberries fills these pretty wreaths.

1	recipe *Enriched Egg Dough* (page 30)
1	cup finely chopped fresh or frozen cranberries
½	cup frozen raspberries
½	cup sugar
1½	teaspoons grated orange peel
1	egg beaten with 1 tablespoon milk
	Coarse or pearl sugar

❶ Prepare dough as directed. While in first rising, prepare cran-raspberry filling: In medium saucepan, combine cranberries, raspberries, ½ cup sugar and orange peel. Bring to a boil over medium heat. Reduce heat to low; simmer, stirring frequently, 5 minutes or until very thick. Remove from heat; cool.

❷ After first rising of dough, punch down. Turn out onto lightly floured surface. Roll to 21x12-inch rectangle. Spread filling over dough to within ½ inch of edges. Fold lengthwise in thirds, to enclose filling, making 12x7-inch rectangle. Press edges to seal.

❸ Cut dough with pizza wheel or sharp knife into 12 (1-inch) strips. Holding ends of each strip, twist three times. Pinch together ends of each twisted strip to form wreaths; place on greased baking sheets. Cover; let rise in warm place 30 to 45 minutes or until doubled in size.

❹ Heat oven to 400°F. Brush wreaths with egg mixture and sprinkle with coarse sugar. Bake 12 to 15 minutes or until golden brown. Cool on wire racks.

12 servings.

Preparation time: 1 hour, 15 minutes.

Ready to serve: 3 hours, 30 minutes.

Per serving: 425 calories, 14.5 g total fat (8 g saturated fat), 135 mg cholesterol, 35 mg sodium, 2.5 g fiber.

BAKER'S NOTES

• Cranberries are a North American native that grow in bogs, primarily in the Northeast and Upper Midwest, and are related to the blueberry. They keep well in the freezer, so stock up when they're available fresh in the fall.

• Cranberries chop well in the blender when they're partially frozen.

EASTER BABKA

Babka or babke are yeast-batter coffee cakes from Russia, perfect for holiday mornings spent with family and friends. The light, slightly crumbly texture is created by allowing the sponge and batter to rise before baking.

CAKE

1	(¼-oz.) pkg. active dry yeast
¾	cup sugar
1	cup warm milk (105°F to 115°F)
¼	teaspoon salt
3¾	cups unbleached all-purpose flour
½	cup butter
3	eggs, slightly beaten
½	cup dark or golden raisins
1	tablespoon grated lemon peel

STREUSEL

¼	cup packed brown sugar
2	tablespoons unbleached all-purpose flour
¾	teaspoon ground ginger
¼	cup chopped walnuts
1	tablespoon melted butter

TOPPING

2	tablespoons melted butter
⅓	cup apricot preserves, warmed

❶ In medium bowl, dissolve yeast and 1 teaspoon of the sugar in milk; let stand 5 minutes. Stir in salt and 1 cup of the flour; beat well. Cover; let sponge rise in warm place 1 hour or until nearly bubbly and risen.

❷ In large bowl, beat remaining sugar and ½ cup butter until creamy. Beat in eggs and sponge mixture until smooth. Stir in raisins, lemon peel and remaining 2¾ cups flour; mix until smooth, thick batter forms. Cover; let rise 1 hour or until doubled in size.

❸ Grease 10-inch tube pan with removable bottom. Scrape batter into pan. Cover; let rise 30 to 45 minutes or until doubled in size.

❹ Meanwhile, prepare streusel: Mix brown sugar, 2 tablespoons flour, ginger, walnuts and 1 tablespoon melted butter until crumbly.

❺ Heat oven to 350°F. Brush cake with 2 tablespoons melted butter; sprinkle with streusel. Bake 35 to 40 minutes or until light golden brown. Remove from pan; cool on wire rack. Drizzle with warm preserves.

16 servings.
Preparation time: 3 hours, 15 minutes.
Ready to serve: 4 hours, 20 minutes.
Per serving: 295 calories, 10.5 g total fat (5.5 g saturated fat), 60 mg cholesterol, 115 mg sodium, 1.5 g fiber.

BAKER'S NOTE

• Yeasted coffee cakes can be baked in a variety of pans or molds. If you have decorative cake pans or Bundt cake molds, consider using them for special occasion baking. For a Bundt-style pan, sprinkle streusel in the bottom of the pan before pouring in batter. Unmold the coffee cake after baking, inverting it onto a serving plate.

$\mathcal{H}$OT CROSS BUNS

A Good Friday tradition in the Christian church, these tender white sweet buns are laced with ground mace and studded with sweet sherry-macerated currants.

BUNS

¾	cup currants or raisins
⅓	cup cream (sweet) sherry
1	(¼-oz.) pkg. active dry yeast
1¼	cups warm milk (105°F to 115°F)
⅓	cup sugar
¼	cup butter, softened
¾	teaspoon ground mace
½	teaspoon salt
2	eggs

4¼ to 4¾	cups unbleached all-purpose flour
1	egg beaten with 2 teaspoons honey

SHERRY ICING

1	cup powdered sugar
1 to 3	tablespoons cream (sweet) sherry
½	teaspoon vanilla

❶ In small bowl, combine currants and ⅓ cup sherry. Let stand 30 minutes; drain well. In large bowl, dissolve yeast in milk; let stand 5 minutes. Stir in ⅓ cup sugar, butter, mace, salt, eggs and 4 cups of the flour; beating well until soft dough forms. Turn dough out onto lightly floured surface. Knead in enough remaining flour to make moderately soft dough, about 5 minutes. Knead in currants. Place dough in greased bowl; turn dough greased side up. Cover; let rise in warm place 1 hour or until doubled in size.

❷ Line large baking sheets with parchment paper. Punch dough down; turn out onto lightly floured surface. Lightly roll dough into cylinder. Slice into 18 equal pieces; shape into balls by rolling pieces between cupped hands, tucking under sides, pinching seams together at bottom. Place dough on baking sheets. Cover; let rise 35 minutes or until nearly doubled in size.

❸ Heat oven to 400°F. Snip a deep cross in top center of each bun; brush with egg mixture. Bake 10 to 12 minutes or until golden brown; let cool 15 minutes.

❹ Meanwhile, prepare icing: In medium bowl, mix powdered sugar, 1 to 3 tablespoons sherry and vanilla until smooth. Icing should be stiff enough to hold its shape on each bun. Pipe icing into lines of cross snipped on top of each bun. Serve warm.

18 servings.
Preparation time: 1 hours, 45 minutes.
Ready to serve: 2 hours, 30 minutes.
Per serving: 215 calories, 4 g total fat (2 g saturated fat), 40 mg cholesterol, 100 mg sodium, 1 g fiber.

BAKER'S NOTES

- To ice the crosses easily, put icing in a small squeeze bottle, pastry bag with a small tip or a small plastic bag with a corner snipped off.

- Mace is the lacy covering of the nutmeg seed. Its taste is pleasingly peppery and cinnamon-like. A somewhat old-fashioned spice, its unique flavor holds well when stored, unlike other ground spices.

FESTIVE PANETTONE

A specialty of Milan, Italy, panettone *is popular during the Christmas season, but is also on the scene for other special occasions, like weddings and christenings. Serve it for breakfast or dessert ... and day-old panettone makes great bread pudding.*

4 to 4½ cups unbleached all-purpose
       flour
  ½ cup sugar
  1 (¼-oz.) pkg. active dry yeast
  1 tablespoon grated lemon peel
  1 teaspoon anise seeds
  ½ teaspoon salt
  1 cup milk
  ¼ cup water

  ½ cup butter, cut into pieces
  2 eggs
  1 cup snipped dried apricots or
       cherries
  ½ cup pine nuts, plus additional for
       sprinkling
  ½ cup chopped bittersweet chocolate
  1 egg beaten with 1 tablespoon water
    Coarse or pearl sugar

❶ In large bowl, combine 1½ cups of the flour, ½ cup sugar, yeast, lemon peel, anise and salt. In medium saucepan, heat milk, water and butter together until very warm (120°F to 130°F). Slowly stir into dry ingredients; beat with electric mixer at medium speed. Beat in eggs and ½ cup of the flour 2 minutes at high speed.

❷ Generously grease 2 (11.5- to 13-oz.) coffee cans or 1 (2-lb.) coffee can. By hand, stir in enough remaining flour to make stiff batter. Cover; let rise in warm place 1 hour or until doubled in size. Stir batter down. Add apricots, ½ cup pine nuts and chocolate; mix well.

❸ Spoon batter into can(s). Cover; let rise 30 to 45 minutes or until batter is doubled in size (or up to within ½ inch of top of cans).

❹ Heat oven to 350°F. Brush dough with egg mixture; sprinkle with pine nuts and coarse sugar. Bake on lowest oven rack 35 minutes for smaller cans or 40 to 45 minutes for large can, until browned and wooden skewer inserted into bread comes out clean.

8 or 16 servings.
Preparation time: 2 hours.
Ready to serve: 3 hours, 15 minutes.
Per serving: 280 calories, 11.5 g total fat (5.5 g saturated fat), 55 mg cholesterol, 135 mg sodium, 2.5 g fiber.

BAKER'S NOTES

• Coffee cans, a convenient way to make upright loaves, come in different sizes and weights. Look for cans that will hold either 4 cups (11.5 to 13 oz.) or 8 cups (2 lb.).

• Pine nuts (also known as *pignoli or piñons*) are expensive, cream-colored, drop-shaped nuts. They're harvested from certain pine trees in the southwestern U.S., Mexico and the Mediterranean. Rich in flavor but high in fat, they should be stored in the refrigerator.

SPICED PUMPKIN BREAD

A fall baking classic, this quick loaf can be made with freshly cooked and pureed pumpkin, winter squash or sweet potatoes. The fresh, deep spiciness of these loaves is irresistible, redolent of freshly grated and crystallized ginger, and cinnamon. Make these smaller loaves for gift giving.

BREAD

- 1 cup packed brown sugar
- 1 cup vegetable oil
- 1½ cups canned pumpkin puree
- ½ cup chopped crystallized (candied) ginger
- 4 eggs
- 2 teaspoons grated fresh ginger
- 2 cups unbleached all-purpose flour
- 1 cup whole wheat flour
- 2 teaspoons baking soda
- 2 teaspoons baking powder
- 1 teaspoon ground cinnamon
- ½ teaspoon salt
- 1 cup dried cranberries, chopped hulled pumpkin seeds or toasted pine nuts

GLAZE

- ½ cup orange marmalade, warmed
- 2 tablespoons orange-flavored liqueur or orange juice
- 2 tablespoons powdered sugar

❶ Heat oven to 350°F. Grease 4 (5x3-inch) mini loaf pans. In large bowl, combine brown sugar, oil, pumpkin, ginger and eggs; blend well.

❷ In medium bowl, stir together all-purpose flour, whole wheat flour, baking soda, baking powder, cinnamon and salt. Stir dry ingredients into wet ingredients, just until moistened. Fold in dried cranberries.

❸ Pour batter into pans. Bake 45 minutes or until wooden pick inserted in center comes out clean. Cool 10 minutes; remove from pans. Cool completely on wire rack.

❹ Meanwhile, prepare glaze: Combine marmalade, orange liqueur and powdered sugar. Drizzle glaze over cooled breads.

20 servings.

Preparation time: 25 minutes.

Ready to serve: 2 hours, 15 minutes.

Per serving: 285 calories, 12 g total fat (2 g saturated fat), 45 mg cholesterol, 265 mg sodium, 2 g fiber.

BAKER'S NOTES

- Because crystallized ginger is sticky when chopped, mix it in with the wet ingredients so it will be more evenly distributed in the bread batter.
- Try using a combination of dried fruit and nuts in these loaves. Dried cranberries and pine nuts are a complementary combination.
- To grate fresh ginger, peel skin from the ginger knob, unless it's very young and has tender skin. Rub peeled ginger against a fine metal grater, microplane or one of the special ceramic ginger graters from Asia. Fresh ginger can be kept on hand in the freezer, wrapped in plastic wrap. But it is also conveniently available finely grated in small jars — look in the produce section. And of course, a teaspoon of dried ginger can be used in a pinch.

$\mathscr{N}$ORWEGIAN YULEKAGE

A favorite in Denmark and Sweden, as well as Norway, this Christmas loaf is defined by the liberal use of ground cardamom and candied and dried fruit.

2 (¼-oz.) pkg. active dry yeast	4 to 4¾ cups unbleached all-purpose flour
1 cup warm milk (105°F to 115°F)	1 cup chopped mixed candied fruit
¼ cup butter, softened	
½ cup sugar	½ cup golden raisins
2 eggs	1 egg beaten with 1 teaspoon water
2 teaspoons freshly ground cardamom	
¼ teaspoon ground cinnamon	1 recipe *Almond Glaze* (page 41)
½ teaspoon salt	

❶ In small bowl, dissolve yeast in milk. In large bowl, beat butter, sugar and eggs together until smooth. Beat in yeast mixture, cardamom, cinnamon, salt and enough of the flour to make soft dough (about 4 cups).

❷ Turn dough out onto floured surface. Knead 5 minutes, adding more flour as needed to prevent sticking. Cover; let rest 15 minutes. Pat dough out to make rough rectangle; sprinkle with candied fruit and raisins. Fold dough over fruit, kneading until fruit is evenly distributed. Place in greased bowl; turn dough greased side up. Cover; let rise in warm place 1 hour or until doubled in size.

❸ Grease 2 (9x5-inch) loaf pans. Punch dough down. Divide dough in half; shape into loaves. Place in pans. Cover; let rise 1 hour or until doubled in size.

❹ Heat oven to 375°F. Snip top of dough decoratively with kitchen shears; brush with egg mixture. Bake 23 to 28 minutes or until golden brown. Remove from pans; cool on wire rack. Drizzle with glaze.

24 servings.
Preparation time: 2 hours, 50 minutes.
Ready to serve: 4 hours, 15 minutes.
Per serving: 175 calories, 5 g total fat (2.5 g saturated fat), 35 mg cholesterol, 110 mg sodium, 1 g fiber.

VARIATION   Pistacio-Cranberry Yulekage
Substitute chopped pistachios for the candied fruit and dried cranberries for the raisins. After first rising, divide dough in half. Roll each half into 18- to 20-inch rope. Twist ropes together; place on greased baking sheet and form into a wreath. Let rise once more, brush with egg mixture and bake as directed.

$\mathcal{A}$ROMATIC SEEDED CHALLAH

Challah (pronounced Ha-la), the traditional Jewish sabbath bread, is a lovely braided loaf made from a light egg dough. Sometimes the bread is shaped into a circle, coil or a bird-like shape; each is symbolic of a different Jewish holiday or significant historical event.

BREAD

1   (¼-oz.) pkg. active dry yeast or 2¼ teaspoons bread machine yeast

2   cups unbleached all-purpose flour or bread flour

1   cup whole wheat flour

1   teaspoon salt

2   tablespoons honey

1   tablespoon olive oil

1   egg

1   cup lukewarm water

1   egg yolk beaten with 1 teaspoon water

SEED TOPPING

1   teaspoon poppy seeds

1   teaspoon sesame seeds

½   teaspoon fennel seeds

½   teaspoon caraway seeds

⅛   teaspoon celery, cumin or dill seeds

❶ Place yeast, all-purpose flour, whole wheat flour, salt, honey, oil, egg and water in 1½-lb. loaf bread machine, following manufacturer's instructions. Select Dough cycle; press Start.

❷ Remove dough from machine when cycle is finished; let rest 10 minutes.

❸ Grease large baking sheet. Turn dough out onto lightly floured surface; knead dough 30 seconds. Divide into 3 equal pieces; roll each into 15- to 18-inch rope. Braid 3 ropes together; seal ends. Place on baking sheet. Cover; let rise 30 to 40 minutes or until doubled in size. Mix poppy, sesame, fennel, caraway and celery seeds.

❹ Heat oven to 375°F. Brush dough with egg yolk mixture; sprinkle with seed mixture. Bake 20 to 25 minutes or until loaf sounds hollow when lightly tapped. Cool on wire rack.

12 servings.

Preparation time: 2 hours.

Ready to serve: 3 hours, 20 minutes.

Per serving: 145 calories, 2.5 g total fat (0.5 g saturated fat), 35 mg cholesterol, 200 mg sodium, 2 g fiber.

BAKER'S NOTES

• Seed and spice mixtures stirred into dough make interesting seasonings for baking. They also add a bite and a burst of flavor when sprinkled on crusts. The seed topping for this bread can be varied to your personal taste — keep your favorite combination on hand for other breads or rolls. Be sure to store all seeds in a cool, dry place.

• This dough can be mixed in the food processor.

• To make a ring or wreath, roll the ropes of dough to 24 inches in length.

ORANGE-CINNAMON BRIOCHE

Brioche is classically French. It's truly a cross between bread and cake.

2 (¼-oz.) pkg. active dry yeast
¼ cup warm water (105°F to 115°F)
½ cup warm milk (105°F to 115°F)
2 tablespoons sugar
2 tablespoons grated orange peel
1½ teaspoons ground cinnamon

1 teaspoon salt
4½ to 5 cups unbleached all-purpose flour
1 cup butter, softened
6 eggs
2 egg yolks beaten with 2
teaspoons milk

❶ In large bowl, dissolve yeast in water; let stand 5 minutes. Stir in milk, sugar, orange peel, cinnamon and salt. Beat in 2 cups of the flour; add butter and continue beating until well blended.

❷ Stir in eggs, one at a time. Add remaining 2½ cups flour. Beat dough in bowl with spoon until it becomes difficult, then work with hands 15 to 20 minutes in bowl or turn out onto generously floured surface to knead until shiny and elastic. Cover bowl; let rise in warm place 2 hours or until nearly tripled in volume. (Dough can be made up to this point; refrigerate overnight if desired.)

❸ Punch dough down. Reserve about ⅕ of dough; divide remainder into 24 pieces. Shape into smooth balls (about 1½-inches in diameter) between cupped hands. Place each ball in (2½-inch) muffin cup or (3½-inch) fluted tart mold or brioche tin.

❹ Divide reserved dough into 24 (¾-inch) balls. With a forefinger dipped in water, press indentation into center of each larger ball. Place smaller ball into each indentation. Cover; let rise 30 to 40 minutes or until doubled in size.

❺ Heat oven to 425°F. Brush each roll with egg yolk mixture. If using individual tins, place on baking sheet. Bake 15 to 20 minutes or until golden brown. Cool 5 minutes; remove from pans. Serve warm.

24 servings.
Preparation time: 4 hours.
Ready to serve: 4 hours, 35 minutes.
Per serving: 185 calories, 9.5 g total fat (5.5 g saturated fat), 90 mg cholesterol, 170 mg sodium, 1 g fiber.

BAKER'S NOTES

• To toast hazelnuts, place them in a pan in a 350°F oven for 15 minutes. Cool slightly, then rub nuts gently in a kitchen towel to remove most of the papery, mildly bitter skin. This enhances the nuts' rich, buttery flavor.

CHRISTMAS STOLLEN

One of the most famous Christmas breads from Germany, stollen is often given as a gift.

½ cup each milk, water
¼ cup butter, softened
3¼ to 4 cups unbleached all-purpose flour
1 (¼-oz.) pkg. active dry yeast
½ cup sugar
1 teaspoon grated lemon peel
½ teaspoon salt
2 eggs

¼ cup each chopped toasted slivered almonds, finely chopped candied citron, finely chopped candied orange peel, chopped candied cherries
¾ teaspoon freshly grated nutmeg or ground cinnamon
1 egg white, beaten
1 recipe *Vanilla Glaze* (page 41) or powdered sugar
Toasted sliced almonds

❶ In small saucepan, combine milk, water and 3 tablespoons of the butter. Heat mixture until very warm (120°F to 130°F). In large bowl, combine 3 cups of the flour, yeast, ⅓ cup of the sugar, lemon peel and salt. Stir warm liquid and eggs into dry ingredients; beat well. Stir in chopped almonds, citron, orange peel, cherries and enough flour to make soft dough.

❷ Turn dough out onto lightly floured surface. Knead 6 to 8 minutes, adding as much remaining flour as needed to prevent sticking, until smooth and elastic. Place in greased bowl; turn dough greased side up. Cover; let rise in warm place 1 hour or until doubled in size.

❸ Grease large baking sheet. Punch dough down; turn out onto lightly floured surface. Pat dough into oval shape, ½ inch thick. Spread half of oval with remaining 1 tablespoon butter. Sprinkle with remaining sugar and nutmeg. Fold dough in half lengthwise, slightly off-center, so top layer is set back ½ inch from bottom edge; pinch to seal. Place on baking sheet. Cover; let rise 30 to 45 minutes or until doubled in size.

❹ Heat oven to 350°F. Brush dough with egg white. Bake 30 to 35 minutes or until golden brown. Cool completely on wire rack. Drizzle with glaze or dust with powdered sugar; sprinkle with sliced almonds.

16 servings.
Preparation time: 2 hours, 20 minutes.
Ready to serve: 3 hours, 50 minutes.
Per serving: 225 calories, 5 g total fat (2.5 g saturated fat), 35 mg cholesterol, 135 mg sodium, 1 g fiber.

BAKER'S NOTE

• What's citron? A very tart citrus fruit that's never eaten raw because it's too sour and bitter. But its peel is candied and used in baked goods (especially fruitcakes). It's usually found during the fall baking season with the candied fruits. If citron is unavailable, substitute an equal amount of candied lemon peel and some lemon extract.

RECIPE INDEX

This index lists every recipe in At Home with Bread *by name. If you're looking for a specific recipe but can't recall the exact name, turn to the General Index that starts on page 172.*

GENERAL INDEX

There are several ways to use this helpful index. First — you can find recipes by name. Second — if you don't know a recipe's specific name but recall a special ingredient, or the bread type or baking technique, look under that heading and all the related recipes will be listed; scan for the recipe you want. Finally — you can use this general index to find a summary of the recipes in each chapter of the book (mini breads, quick breads, flat breads, etc.).